P9-AGG-744

CHARACTER ENCYCLOPEDIA
NEW EDITION

WRITTEN BY
ELIZABETH DOWSETT, SIMON HUGO, AND CAVAN SCOTT

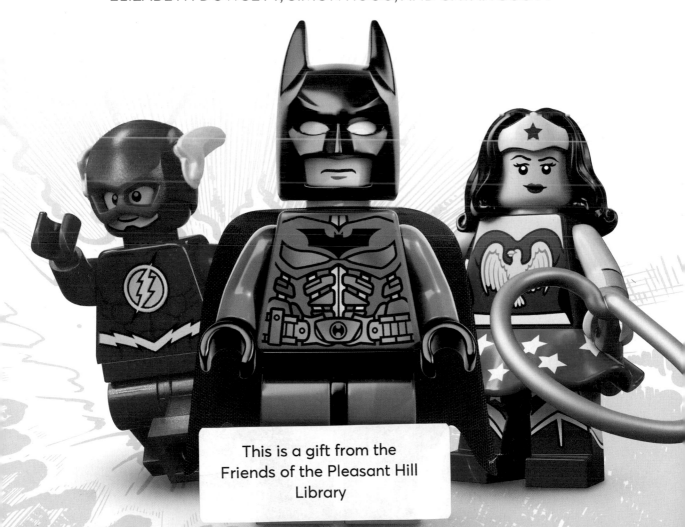

This is a gift from the
Friends of the Pleasant Hill
Library

CONTENTS

JUSTICE LEAGUE BEWARE!

SUPERMAN ARRIVES on Earth from his distant home planet, Krypton. He soon makes friends and allies. The Man of Steel has amazing superpowers, but sometimes it's more than a one-person job keeping Metropolis safe.

COSMIC BOY

SUPERMAN

JOR-EL

LOIS LANE

SUPERGIRL

CLARK KENT

A REPORTER WITH A SECRET

Serious, businesslike hairstyle

Glasses are part of Clark's disguise

Red tie hints at identity

VITAL STATS

LIKES: Reporting stories
DISLIKES: Too many questions
FRIENDS: Lois Lane
FOES: People who are too curious
SKILLS: Keeping secrets, writing stories
GEAR: None

FIRST SET: LEGO® *Batman—The Movie: DC Super Heroes Unite* DVD
SET NUMBER: N/A
YEAR: 2013

REPORTING FOR DUTY

With his work suit discarded, Clark is Superman. Instead of writing stories, he rights wrongs—using his powers to protect the population from threats like Brainiac's scary Skull Ship.

CLARK KENT IS a reporter for the *Daily Planet*. But if he took his glasses off, people would realize he is actually Superman. His minifigure does have another clue—the Kryptonian costume under his office suit.

A determined face—
Superman is ready
to stand for truth
and justice

Eye-catching
red cape

VITAL STATS

LIKES: A peaceful
Metropolis
DISLIKES: Kryptonite
FRIENDS: Wonder Woman
FOES: Lex Luthor
SKILLS: Flight
GEAR: None

FIRST SET: Superman
(NYCC 2011 exclusive)
SET NUMBER:
COMCON017
YEAR: 2011

SILVER KNUCKLE RIDE

The first-ever Superman with
mini legs isn't short on fighting
skills. He can still pack a punch
against Bizarro in his Mighty
Micros car, which has its own fists
for delivering the message.

Superman's
yellow belt is
also printed
on his back

THE LAST SURVIVOR of the
doomed planet Krypton, Superman
was rocketed to Earth as a baby.
Powered by the sun, the Man of
Steel can fly faster than a speeding
bullet, lift incredible weights, and
fire lasers from his eyes.

VITAL STATS

LIKES: Metropolis
DISLIKES: Falling structures
FRIENDS: Moviegoers
FOES: General Zod
SKILLS: Heat vision
GEAR: None

FIRST SET: Superman:
Metropolis Showdown
SET NUMBER: 76002
YEAR: 2013

Suit is modeled on traditional Kryptonian clothing, worn under battle armor on Superman's home planet

DID YOU KNOW?

In the early 1990s, Superman wore a black costume with a chrome crest in DC comic books.

Top of cape is now printed on torso

Suit detailing is also printed on the legs

THE MAN IN BLACK

This somber version of the *Man of Steel* minifigure was won by 200 lucky raffle winners at San Diego Comic-Con in 2013. His black outfit signifies his nightmare while captured in the Black Zone.

IN A DARKER BLUE outfit, this more modern-looking Superman has rid himself of the red shorts over his tights. Released to tie in with the *Man of Steel* movie, he is angry at the villainous Zod threatening Metropolis and Smallville.

SUPERMAN
SUITED AND REBOOTED

THE MAN of Steel has experimented with a few different looks over the years, but he tends to stick with his trademark red and blue colors for his Kryptonian costume.

New tousled hair piece

Dual-molded legs with red boots

VITAL STATS

LIKES: Heights
DISLIKES: Kryptonite
FRIENDS: Lois Lane, Batman, Wonder Woman
FOES: Lex Luthor
SKILLS: Flight
GEAR: None

FIRST SET: Heroes of Justice: Sky High Battle
SET NUMBER: 76046
YEAR: 2016

VITAL STATS

LIKES: Rescue dogs
DISLIKES: Kryptonite prisons
FRIENDS: Krypto the Super-Dog
FOES: Lobo
SKILLS: Super-strength
GEAR: None

FIRST SET: Superman & Krypto Team-Up
SET NUMBER: 76096
YEAR: 2018

All Superman minifigures have this hair piece or the one with the curl

Shorts are back outside tights

Cape with a single hole

VITAL STATS

LIKES: Good news stories
DISLIKES: Bad press
FRIENDS: *Daily Planet* readers
FOES: Liars
SKILLS: Making headlines
GEAR: *Daily Planet* newspaper

FIRST SET: Collectible LEGO® DC Super Heroes Minifigures Series
SET NUMBER: 71026
YEAR: 2020

Headline reads "Caped Wonder Stuns City."

LOIS LANE
DAILY PLANET REPORTER

VITAL STATS

LIKES: Following leads
DISLIKES: Being kidnapped
FRIENDS: Superman
FOES: General Zod
SKILLS: Investigating, escaping from aliens
GEAR: None

FIRST SET: Superman: Black Zero Escape
SET NUMBER: 76009
YEAR: 2013

Exclusive head available only on this minifigure

Long red hair piece shared with Mera, Batgirl, and a version of The Cheetah minifigures

Printed blouse and vest is suitable attire for a newshound

Practical blue pants

ESCAPE POD PERIL
Is it any wonder the other side of Lois's head has a terrified expression? She's launched out of General Zod's Black Zero ship in an escape pod!

DID YOU KNOW?
This Lois Lane minifigure is based on her appearance in the 2013 *Man of Steel* movie.

INTREPID REPORTER Lois Lane knew she had a story on her hands from the moment the first reports about Superman came in. Following her leads, she tracked the Man of Steel to his Smallville home and discovered his secret identity.

LOIS LANE
STAR OF THE *DAILY PLANET*

Serious face can be swapped for scared look

Camera for capturing breaking news

Smart suit for doing interviews

ACE NEWS REPORTER
Lois Lane knows Superman's secret, but he trusts her not to print it in the *Daily Planet*! With a camera in her hand and a big story in her sights, there's nowhere Lois won't go to find the facts for tomorrow's headlines.

A NOSE FOR NEWS
Lois loves to investigate and often gets into danger following her reporter's instincts. When she starts to ask questions about Lex Luthor, she ends up hanging from his helicopter!

LEXCORP

VITAL STATS

LIKES: Exclusives
DISLIKES: Cover-ups
FRIENDS: Superman
FOES: Lex Luthor
SKILLS: Getting to the truth
GEAR: Camera

FIRST SET: Heroes of Justice: Sky High Battle
SET NUMBER: 76046
YEAR: 2016

15

JOR-EL

SUPERMAN'S FATHER

VITAL STATS

LIKES: Science
DISLIKES: The Kryptonian Council
FRIENDS: His wife
FOES: General Zod
SKILLS: Genetic manipulation
GEAR: None

FIRST SET: Jor-El
SET NUMBER: 5001623
YEAR: 2013

DID YOU KNOW?

This minifigure is based on the 2013 *Man of Steel* movie. It was given free to customers at shop.LEGO.com and LEGO® stores when the movie was released.

Armor detailing is similar to Superman's *Man of Steel* variant

The "S" symbol means "hope" in Kryptonian

While Superman's armor is gold in tones, Jor-El's is bronze

FROM FATHER TO SON

As "Clark Kent," Superman discovered a Kryptonian spaceship on Earth. From it, a holographic image of Jor-El appeared to teach Clark about his alien heritage and present the Last Son of Krypton with his Superman uniform.

WHEN CHIEF SCIENTIST Jor-El realized that his planet, Krypton, was about to explode, he tried to warn the Kryptonian High Council. When his advice was ignored, Jor-El sent his son to Earth for safety. This son would become Superman!

Bald head for this bold hero

DID YOU KNOW?
Colonel Hardy shares a head with the Bank Guard from The Batmobile and the Two-Face Chase (set 8684).

Pockets to store ammo

VITAL STATS

LIKES: United States Air Force
DISLIKES: Helicopters
FRIENDS: Superman, Lois Lane
FOES: General Zod, Faora
SKILLS: Pilot
GEAR: None

FIRST SET: Superman: Battle of Smallville
SET NUMBER: 76003
YEAR: 2013

Radio to call for backup

GETTING THE DROP ON ZOD
Colonel Hardy becomes a hero when he stages an attack on Zod's spacecraft. He triggers a portal that drags the ship back to the Phantom Zone, proving that the mighty Dropship is no match for the nifty offroader.

A MEMBER OF THE US Air Force, Colonel Nathan Hardy was ordered to bring down the battling Kryptonians that were flattening Smallville. However, the Colonel realized that the Man of Steel wasn't their enemy after Superman saved his life.

CAPED COUSIN

WHAT DO YOU GET when you cross superpowers with teenage attitude? Plenty of trouble, that's what! Sent to Earth to care for her cousin Kal-El, Kara Zor-El's spacecraft was knocked off course. She actually arrives years after Superman has grown up!

Long flowing blonde hair

Supergirl's torso has been adjusted especially for her and is exclusive to this variant

DID YOU KNOW?

Supergirl made her first appearance in a 1959 issue of *Action Comics*.

RARE RAFFLE PRIZE

This Supergirl minifigure was intended for San Diego Comic-Con 2020. When the event was canceled, the exclusive minifgure was raffled off to lucky winners at the DC Virtual FanDome event instead.

VITAL STATS

LIKES: Flying into action
DISLIKES: Rules
FRIENDS: Superman, Martian Manhunter
FOES: Brainiac
SKILLS: Heat vision, super-strength
GEAR: None

FIRST SET: Brainiac Attack
SET NUMBER: 76040
YEAR: 2015

SUPERBOY

THE BOY OF STEEL

Tousled dark hair

Rare two-tone minifigure arms gives T-shirt effect

Muscle tone shows through tight shirt

Blue jeans show Superboy's casual approach to costumes

DID YOU KNOW?

Superboy's first LEGO appearance was in the video game LEGO® Batman™ 2: DC Super Heroes, where he wore an all-black outfit.

A LIKELY LAD

In 2015, exclusive set 5004077 revealed another Super Hero from faraway: Lightning Lad. This character's ability to create eletricity is shown with the dramatic lightning bolts on his minifigure's torso and legs.

VITAL STATS

LIKES: Being a hero
DISLIKES: Being called Superboy
FRIENDS: Superman
FOES: Lex Luthor
SKILLS: Flight, super-strength
GEAR: Doesn't need any!

FIRST SET: Minifigure Gift Set
SET NUMBER: 5004076
YEAR: 2014

CONNER KENT was cloned from Lex Luthor and Superman's DNA but still became Superman's pal, earning the Kryptonian name Kon-El. He has similar abilities to Superman, such as super-strength, heat vision, X-ray vision, freeze breath, and flight.

COSMIC BOY

MASTER OF MAGNETISM

COSMIC BOY

VITAL STATS

LIKES: Heavy metal
DISLIKES: Electromagnetic interference
FRIENDS: Superman, Lightning Lad
FOES: Brainiac
SKILLS: Super-magnetism, leadership
GEAR: Magnetic fields

FIRST SET: Cosmic Boy
SET NUMBER: 30604
YEAR: 2016

Slicked-back hair piece shared with Bruce Wayne and General Zod

DID YOU KNOW?
Cosmic Boy's minifigure also came with the Blu-Ray and DVD release of the movie LEGO® DC Comics™ Super Heroes Justice League: Cosmic Clash.

Discs can be removed and used as weapons

Hands can create blasts and short-circuit electrical machines

RIDING THE WAVES
On Earth, Cosmic Boy can fly by riding the planet's magnetic fields. The young hero can also condense magnetic energy into powerful concussive blasts. Pow!

ROKK KRINN'S KNACK for manipulating magnetic fields is impressive, even by the high standards of his home planet, Braal. As Cosmic Boy, he can bend metal—even the iron in people's blood—to his will.

VAL-ZOD

EARTH-2 SUPERMAN

First Superman minifigure to wear a white cape

VAL-ZOD IS THE second man to flee Krypton's destruction, find refuge on an Earth, and wear the old red and blues to protect his adopted planet. Anything the first Superman can do, Val-Zod can do, too. Just as super, he has all the same powers—and all the same weaknesses.

Background color is red instead of the "S"

Tall white boots

VITAL STATS

LIKES: Encyclopedias
DISLIKES: Open spaces
FRIENDS: Supergirl, Wonders of the World
FOES: Anyone threatening Earth-2
SKILLS: Superhuman powers
GEAR: None

FIRST SET: LEGO DC *Character Encyclopedia Updated Edition*
SET NUMBER: N/A
YEAR: 2022

CATCHING RAYS

As a typical Kryptonian, Val-Zod gains powers from the solar radiation of a "yellow" sun. His powers include flight, superhuman strength, and x-ray and heat vision, but he is vulnerable to Kryptonite.

21

CHAPTER TWO
SUPERMAN'S ENEMIES

LEX LUTHOR

LOBO

TOR-AN

SOMEONE GIVE
ME A WEAPON!

GENERAL ZOD

METROPOLIS IS A dangerous place.
Superman and his allies have their work
cut out keeping the city safe from all
the looney lawbreakers, evil geniuses,
and violent savages. And then there
are those who just really don't like him.
For some criminals, it's personal.

LEX LUTHOR

LEXCORP LEADER

VITAL STATS

LIKES: Having hair, helicopters
DISLIKES: Super Hero team-ups
FRIENDS: Henchman
FOES: Superman, Wonder Woman, Batman
SKILLS: Computer coding
GEAR: LexCorp helicopter

FIRST SET: Heroes of Justice: Sky High Battle
SET NUMBER: 76046
YEAR: 2016

Unusually, this Lex minifigure has locks

Smart-casual sand-colored clothes of a tech company boss

EVIL GENIUS

Lex Luthor is a master inventor. An earlier black-suited (and bald!) Lex built Kryptonite-powered battle armor to defeat Superman once and for all. The bait in his trap? None other than Wonder Woman herself!

LEX LUTHOR IS Superman's archnemesis in the city of Metropolis. His 2016 minifigure luxuriates in long hair and a leisure suit, but there's nothing relaxed about his grimace, which he uses to menace Lois Lane.

LEX LUTHOR
SUPERMAN'S GREATEST ENEMY

MEAN, GREEN MACHINE

In his robotic vehicle, Lex wears a warsuit with bright-green collared armor. His first minifigure to wear it was a 2012 giveaway at GameStop stores with preorders of LEGO® Batman™ 2: DC Super Heroes.

Power actuator

Armored segments cover muscles

High-tech power suit gives Lex his powers

VITAL STATS

LIKES: Kryptonite
DISLIKES: Red-caped Super Heroes
FRIENDS: Cheetah
FOES: Batman, Wonder Woman, Firestorm
SKILLS: Great intelligence
GEAR: Mech with escape pod

FIRST SET: Lex Luthor Mech Takedown
SET NUMBER: 76097
YEAR: 2018

REALIZING THAT HE is physically no match for Superman, billionaire businessman Lex Luthor uses his vast resources to design powerful armor. Lex's new gadget is capable of flight and can boost his strength to super-human levels.

25

DID YOU KNOW?

This figure was given away with some preorders of the LEGO® *DC Super-Villains* video game.

Previous Luthor head piece shows it really is him

Luthor's take on the Superman logo

VITAL STATS

LIKES: Redemption
DISLIKES: Anyone threatening Metropolis
FRIENDS: Superman
FOES: Criminals
SKILLS: An inventive mind
GEAR: None

FIRST SET: Lex Luthor
SET NUMBER: 30614
YEAR: 2018

A HEAD FOR HEIGHTS

With only his wits to help him, Luthor uses his technological know-how to give him an edge over opponents. He borrows more from Superman than just style—his suit also gives him the power of flight.

Additional high-tech improvements

Same LEGO® cape as worn by Superman

IF YOU CAN'T beat them, join them! After a career of fighting Super Heroes, Luthor dons his own red cape and a warsuit styled after Superman's outfit. He uses his genius to fight crime in Metropolis, even joining forces with the Man of Steel against common enemies.

GENERAL ZOD

KRYPTONIAN CRIMINAL

VITAL STATS

LIKES: Making war
DISLIKES: The Phantom Zone
FRIENDS: Faora, Tor-An
FOES: Superman, Colonel Hardy
SKILLS: Super-strength and speed
GEAR: Kryptonian helmet

FIRST SET: Superman: Battle of Smallville
SET NUMBER: 76003
YEAR: 2013

DID YOU KNOW?

A General Zod minifigure without his cape and helmet is available in Superman: Metropolis Showdown (set 76002).

Two-sided head featuring heat-vision eyes on the reverse

General Zod's Kryptonian emblem

Black cape

SPACE ARMOR

Following Superman across the galaxy, Zod needs a Kryptonian battle helmet to breathe in Earth's atmosphere. The aliens first clashed in the small town where Clark Kent, aka Superman, grew up—Smallville.

AS THE PLANET KRYPTON ripped itself apart, Zod tried to overthrow the Kryptonian council and take control. Defeated, he and his coconspirators were trapped in the Phantom Zone for all eternity—until Krypton's eventual destruction set them free!

Faora shares hair with Nightwing and Beast Boy

Shock! Faora also shares a two-sided head with Wonder Woman

Hips printed on the minifigure's body

TO SAVE EARTH, Superman surrendered himself to Zod. The triumphant General sent his second-in-command, Faora, to collect the Man of Steel and Lois Lane. Their encounter would lead to a devastating battle in Smallville.

Faora's family crest

VITAL STATS

LIKES: Explosions
DISLIKES: Jor-El and his family
FRIENDS: General Zod, Tor-An
FOES: Superman, Colonel Hardy
SKILLS: Hand-to-hand superpowered combat
GEAR: Kryptonian helmet and weapon

FIRST SET: Superman: Battle of Smallville
SET NUMBER: 76003
YEAR: 2013

SOLAR-POWERED
Like Zod, Faora needs breathing apparatus to survive Earth's atmosphere, but she soon discovers that the solar system's yellow sun grants her new superpowers of her own. She won't be needing her weapon!

TUR-AN
KRYPTONIAN SOLDIER

VITAL STATS

LIKES: Fighting
DISLIKES: The Phantom Zone
FRIENDS: General Zod, Faora
FOES: Superman, Colonel Hardy
SKILLS: Piloting the dropship
GEAR: Kryptonian weapon

FIRST SET: Superman: Battle of Smallville
SET NUMBER: 76003
YEAR: 2013

This minifigure has the same head as Lex Luthor

DID YOU KNOW?
This minifigure has brown hair, like his comic book counterpart, and unlike his black-haired movie character.

Tor-An's Kryptonian emblem

No cape for this pilot—it would only restrict his space in the cockpit

TOO BAD, TOR-AN
As the pilot of the dropship, Tor-An sees all of the action from his domed cockpit. After the battle on Earth, he is banished to the Phantom Zone by Colonel Hardy.

TOR-AN HELPED General Zod track Superman's path through the cosmos to Earth. Genetically engineered to be a soldier and a loyal member of the Kryptonian Warrior Guild, Tor-An is a master of several alien martial arts.

29

NEVER MIND HEROES or villains, good causes or bad causes. The only one Lobo looks out for is himself—and whoever pays him the most. The bounty hunter is an alien Czarnian. He is the last of his kind—he got rid of all the other Czarnians!

Heightened senses

Black version of Aquaman's 2019 hair piece

Alien body can regenerate itself when injured

VITAL STATS

LIKES: High fees
DISLIKES: Teamwork
FRIENDS: None
FOES: Superman, Krypto the Super-Dog
SKILLS: Alien superpowers
GEAR: Space Hog bike

FIRST SET: Superman & Krypto Team-Up
SET NUMBER: 76096
YEAR: 2018

SPACE HOGGER
Lobo has a bone to pick with Superman, and he has locked him in a Kryptonite prison. To rescue him, Superman's dog must get past Lobo in his skull-fronted Space Hog bike.

BRAINIAC

LIVING COMPUTER

AN ALIEN SUPERCOMPUTER

from the planet Colu, Brainiac believes that knowledge is power. In order to understand other races, he steals entire cities, shrinking them to fit into jars—without asking first!

Computer connections

Lime-green skin

Purple wiring printed on both sides of minifigure

VITAL STATS

LIKES: Knowledge
DISLIKES: Kryptonite
FRIENDS: Gorilla Grodd
FOES: Superman, Supergirl, Martian Manhunter
SKILLS: Genius-level intellect
GEAR: Skull ship

FIRST SET: Brainiac Attack
SET NUMBER: 76040
YEAR: 2015

UFO ON THE GO

The Mini Micro Brainiac has little legs but big ambitions to crush Supergirl's rocket with his UFO vehicle. He drives one-handed to keep his clutches on his shrunken city of Kandor.

DID YOU KNOW?

Brainiac turned Supergirl's dad into a cyborg, for the crime of being a native of Kandor City.

CHAPTER THREE

HEROES OF GOTHAM CITY

THE DARK KNIGHT fights crime, but his caped shoulders don't have to carry all the responsibility. Other folks also answer the call. Whether they're battling baddies or preparing Batman's lobster thermidor, they're all heroes of Gotham City.

BATGIRL

ROBIN

SWAT

COMMISSIONER GORDON

BRUCE WAYNE

CRIME-FIGHTING BILLIONAIRE

Slicked-back black hair

Chiseled cheekbones and a serious expression

A stylish sand-blue suit

VITAL STATS

LIKES: The Batcave
DISLIKES: Drill tanks
FRIENDS: Robin
FOES: Poison Ivy, Bane
SKILLS: A quick Bat-change
GEAR: Batphone

FIRST SET: The Batcave
SET NUMBER: 6860
YEAR: 2012

BRUCE IS THE BILLIONAIRE boss of Wayne Industries. He raises money for charity through the Wayne Foundation, throws lavish parties, and is often featured in Gotham City's gossip columns. (He's also secretly Batman—but don't tell anybody!)

DID YOU KNOW?

Bruce's stern expression is similar to the face you'll find under the Batman minifigure's cowl.

BECOMING BATMAN

The first Bruce minifigure has a bridge in his Batcave leading to a chamber where Bruce can change from dark-blue clothes into his Batsuit.

BRUCE WAYNE

THE MAN BEHIND THE MASK

Neat, no-nonsense hair

Stylish cravat under open shirt

Wayne family crest on blazer

VITAL STATS

LIKES: Healthy outdoor pursuits
DISLIKES: Rudeness, cowards
FRIENDS: Dick Grayson, Alfred
FOES: Angling competitors
SKILLS: Public service
GEAR: Batphone

FIRST SET: *Batman Classic TV Series—Batcave*
SET NUMBER: 76052
YEAR: 2016

RED ALERT

As well as being filled with all his sporting trophies, Bruce's study is home to a bright-red telephone. This gives the Gotham City police a direct line to Batman and Robin.

DID YOU KNOW?

The classic Batman TV series ran for three seasons between 1966 and 1968, with a total of 120 episodes!

THE BILLIONAIRE owner of Wayne Manor is also the owner of the high-tech Batcave, which is hidden beneath his stately pile. Bruce is accomplished at riding horseback, fishing, climbing, and marbles. He also cares for his young ward, Dick Grayson.

Plaid jacket in tweed

Simple, swept-back hair

Maroon tie takes inspiration from a 1960s Bruce Wayne outfit

VITAL STATS

LIKES: The Batcave in one piece
DISLIKES: Intruders
FRIENDS: Robin, Batwoman
FOES: Catwoman, Two-Face, Clayface
SKILLS: Keeping a secret
GEAR: Transformation tower in the Batcave

FIRST SET: Batcave Clayface Invasion
SET NUMBER: 76122
YEAR: 2019

RAZZLE-DAZZLE

Not one for keeping a low profile (despite his explosive secret), Bruce loves a big event. He walks the red carpet to dazzle the public with his charisma, winning smile, and bright-white tuxedo.

A TAILORED TWEED SUIT is Bruce Wayne's idea of relaxing leisurewear. The smart business tycoon is ready to chill out at home, but his enemies have other ideas. The Batcave comes under attack—Bruce had better switch to his Batsuit fast.

THE DRIFTER

BRUCE WAYNE UNDERCOVER

BRUCE WAYNE IS the alter ego of Batman, but now he has a second secret identity as well. Abandoning tailoring for tatters, he becomes the Drifter. This unremarkable scruff can go undercover without attracting anyone's attention.

Frowning face keeps people away

Hooded sweatshirt so he can hide his head if needed

Cozy layers keep him warm without a coat

Dirt added intentionally

DID YOU KNOW?
The Drifter disguise appears in the 2022 film *The Batman*.

VITAL STATS

LIKES: Hot showers
DISLIKES: Rain showers
FRIENDS: Batman, Alfred, Commissioner Gordon
FOES: The Riddler, Selina Kyle
SKILLS: Going undercover
GEAR: Secret Batsuit and motorcycle

FIRST SET: Batcave: The Riddler Face-off
SET NUMBER: 76183
YEAR: 2021

UNDETECTED DETECTIVE
The Riddler is on the run, and the Drifter is tracking him. When the game's up, Batman sheds his disguise and zooms after the rogue to take him on a ride to the Batcave jail.

VITAL STATS

LIKES: Dusting and polishing
DISLIKES: Home invasions
FRIENDS: Bruce Wayne,
Dick Grayson
FOES: The Joker
SKILLS: Excellent telephone
manner
GEAR: Batphone

FIRST SET: *Batman*
Classic TV Series—Batcave
SET NUMBER: 76052
YEAR: 2016

White handkerchief in breast pocket

Batphone for receiving calls from Commissioner Gordon

YOU RANG, SIR?

Alfred's daily duties include answering the Batphone. He summons Batman if he is at home and takes messages from Commissioner Gordon if the Caped Crusader is out.

BRUCE

THE STATELY BUTLER of Wayne Manor, Alfred does much more than just answer the Batphone. He is a mechanic, a swordsman, and an archer and has years of wisdom to offer the Dynamic Duo. Batman and Robin would be lost without him!

ALFRED

BATMAN'S BUTLER

VITAL STATS

LIKES: Neatness and order
DISLIKES: Reckless behavior
FRIENDS: Bruce Wayne, Batman
FOES: The Penguin
SKILLS: Acting, medicine
GEAR: None

FIRST SET: Batcave Break-in
SET NUMBER: 70909
YEAR: 2017

Bald patch clips onto minifigure head

Starched winged collar

Fabric extension for tailcoat

SOME ICE, SIR?

When the Batcave is attacked in 2006, Alfred's first minifigure doesn't lose his cool. In fact, he seems positively chilled when Mr. Freeze traps him in a block of ice!

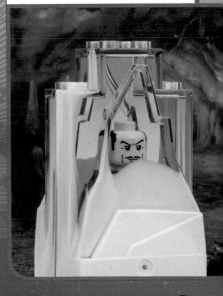

ALFRED PENNYWORTH is one of the few people trusted with Batman's biggest secret: his other identity as Bruce Wayne! He provides loyal service at Wayne Manor—and also beneath it in the Batcave.

ALFRED

GENTLEMAN'S GENTLEMAN

VITAL STATS

LIKES: Driving
DISLIKES: Traffic
FRIENDS: Batman, Robin, Batgirl
FOES: Polka-Dot Man
SKILLS: Activating the Bat-Signal
GEAR: 2 swords

FIRST SET: The Ultimate Batmobile
SET NUMBER: 70917
YEAR: 2017

Batmobile chauffeur's cap

Pencil mustache below bat mask

Alfred's Batsuit is the only one with a starched collar

First batsuit to have a pocket watch

White driving gloves

CAREER FAST TRACK

Working for Batman is a roller-coaster ride. There's never a dull day, and it's probably a bad sign if you're asked to put on a classic Batsuit rather than your traditional butler's uniform.

PART EMPLOYEE, part father figure, Alfred is dedicated to serving Bruce Wayne and Batman. Whether it's driving the Batmobile, waiting on Batman, or changing his whole outfit to be on brand, Alfred's life is all about doing his best.

ALFRED

BATMAN'S RIGHT-HAND MAN

Gray hair piece is worn in black by a 2021 variant of The Penguin

Alfred's minifigure mustache has grown into a beard for the first time

DID YOU KNOW?

This minifigure's design is based on the Alfred who serves *The Batman* in the 2022 film of the same name.

Shirtsleeves are a sign that some serious work is about to be done

VITAL STATS

LIKES: Cleaning and catering

DISLIKES: Messy, unresolved cases

FRIENDS: Batman, the Drifter, Commissioner Gordon

FOES: The Riddler, Selina Kyle

SKILLS: Whatever Batman needs

GEAR: A wide selection of tools

FIRST SET: Batcave: The Riddler Face-off
SET NUMBER: 76183
YEAR: 2021

CLUED-UP

The Riddler's devious deceptions have reached inside the Batcave, which is not okay with Alfred! He helps Batman decipher the clues to tidy up the loose ends of the case.

SOLID AND LEVELHEADED, Alfred supports Batman with a composure as unruffled as his ironed suit. He quietly excels at everything, from adding stains to the Drifter's clothes and welding pieces of the Batcycle together to solving brain teasers.

41

BATMAN
THE MAN IN BLACK

BATMAN IS THE protector of Gotham City. When the Bat-Signal shines in the sky, he answers the call to action—sweeping in from the shadows or blasting onto the scene in his Batmobile.

The first LEGO® Batman cowls have ears going straight up

Armor molded around muscles

Gold Utility Belt can carry grapnel and smoke bombs

VITAL STATS

LIKES: Gotham City
DISLIKES: Crime
FRIENDS: None
FOES: Two-Face
SKILLS: Scaring Super-Villains
GEAR: Batmobile

FIRST SET: The Batmobile: Two Face's Escape
SET NUMBER: 7781
YEAR: 2006

BAT BELT
Batman is a brilliant inventor and his unique Utility Belt is full of gadgets for every occasion. In 2017, his minifigure was given a new piece: a molded, detachable belt that sits between torso and legs.

DID YOU KNOW?
An exclusive San Diego Comic-Con giveaway in 2005 included this first-ever minifigure version of Batman along with The Joker.

BATMAN
THE CAPED CRUSADER

THE DARK Knight updates his outfits as crime-fighting fashion dictates. Blue, black, and gray are his go-to colors, with a belt adding a bit of bling.

Lead-lined cowl

Arched bat-symbol

VITAL STATS

LIKES: Not being seen
DISLIKES: Smiling for photos
FRIENDS: Alfred
FOES: The Joker, Catwoman, Killer Croc
SKILLS: Nighttime camouflage
GEAR: Dragster

FIRST SET: The Batman Dragster: Catwoman Pursuit
SET NUMBER: 7779
YEAR: 2006

VITAL STATS

LIKES: Helping young LEGO® builders
DISLIKES: Complicated Instructions
FRIENDS: Robin
FOES: The Joker
SKILLS: Keeping things simple
GEAR: Batmobile, Batarang

FIRST SET: Batman: Defend the Batcave
SET NUMBER: 10672
YEAR: 2014

VITAL STATS

LIKES: Big pockets for tools
DISLIKES: Criminals running amok in Gotham City
FRIENDS: Robin
FOES: The Riddler, Bane, Scarecrow
SKILLS: Criminology
GEAR: Batcopter, Batarang, Bat-cuffs

FIRST SET: The Batcopter: The Chase for Scarecrow
SET NUMBER: 7786
YEAR: 2007

First blue cowl looks good in the moonlight!

Friendly bright-blue cowl created for LEGO® Juniors sets

Chunky Utility Belt

Simple bat-symbol

Classic bat-symbol on a yellow disc

TRUE OR FALSE?
Batman's first 1960s-inspired minifigure from 2016 has all sorts of high-tech equipment in his Batcave lab. This includes a huge atomic reactor, radar screens, and a lie detector with green and red lights on top.

VITAL STATS

LIKES: Law-abiding citizens
DISLIKES: Dastardly traps
FRIENDS: Robin, Alfred
FOES: The Joker
SKILLS: Science, math, grammar
GEAR: Batarang, Batmobile

FIRST SET: *Batman* Classic TV Series Batmobile
SET NUMBER: 76188
YEAR: 2021

Blue-and-black cowl with printed frown

Bat-symbol on large metallic belt clasp

DID YOU KNOW?
These 2021 and 2016 Batman minifigures are based on his outfit from the *Batman* Classic TV series.

Gray printed tights

IN THE 1960S, clever Batman uses his Bat logic to thwart crafty Super-Villains. He has also even invented a dance called the "Batusi." It helps him keep in shape for his never-ending battle against the rogues of Gotham City!

BATMAN
THE DARK KNIGHT

GOTHAM CITY is becoming more dangerous than ever. The Caped Crusader's Batsuit is becoming more armored, and he has a penchant for dark colors as the Darkest Knight of all.

VITAL STATS

LIKES: Bombing along the road in his new Batmobile
DISLIKES: Bombs on the road
FRIENDS: The Flash
FOES: The Riddler
SKILLS: Racing
GEAR: Batmobile, Batarang

First Batman minifigure with gray gloves

FIRST SET: Batman: The Riddler Chase
SET NUMBER: 76012
YEAR: 2014

VITAL STATS

LIKES: Dangerous missions
DISLIKES: Stolen Kryptonite
FRIENDS: Superman
FOES: LexCorp Henchmen
SKILLS: Recovering Kryptonite
GEAR: Batmobile, silver Batarang

New copper Utility Belt has curvier edges than before

FIRST SET: Kryptonite Interception
SET NUMBER: 76045
YEAR: 2016

Larger bat-symbol

VITAL STATS

LIKES: Armored vehicles
DISLIKES: Panic in the streets
FRIENDS: Jim Gordon
FOES: The Scarecrow
SKILLS: Tumbling
GEAR: Tumbler, grapple hook, Batarang

Black head piece can be swapped for a regular Batman one

FIRST SET: Batmobile Tumbler: Scarecrow Showdown
SET NUMBER: 76239
YEAR: 2021

Costume styled on the movies *Batman v Superman: Dawn of Justice* and *Justice League*

Metallic texture continues on the back of torso

Copper Utility Belt

BATMAN

THE ORIGINAL

VITAL STATS

LIKES: Tights
DISLIKES: Pants
FRIENDS: Classic heroes
FOES: Vintage Super-Villains
SKILLS: Leaping
GEAR: Blue Batarang

FIRST SET: Collectible LEGO DC Super Heroes Minifigures Series
SET NUMBER: 71026
YEAR: 2020

Taller, pointier ears stick out more to the sides

DID YOU KNOW?

Batman's first-ever appearance was in *Detective Comics #27* in May 1939.

Unique blue Batarang

Purple gloves

NEW KNIGHT

In a new costume design, first introduced to the comics in 2011, Batman's 2016 minifigure bites back against Killer Croc in his Bat-Tank. He wears detailed body armor on his front and back.

HEROIC BATMAN dons this classic look from his first comic book appearance. His black-and-gray suit, imposing cape, and sharp ears are more than enough to strike terror into Gotham City's Super-Villain community.

Suit designed by Bruce Wayne to release charge from the front and rear

DID YOU KNOW?

The Electro suit made its first appearance in the LEGO® Batman™ 2: DC Super Heroes video game.

SOMETIMES EVEN

Batman's martial arts aren't enough to bring down Gotham City's Super-Villains. The Dark Knight's Electro suit amps up the action by delivering an electric shock with every punch.

Second type of LEGO cowl has a more curved design around the ears

GLOWERING IN THE DARK

Batman's 2016 minifigure has another specialist suit for the job. Powerful plating protects him in a rooftop clash with Superman. He also has glow-in-the-dark eyes and a hefty bazooka.

VITAL STATS

LIKES: Power
DISLIKES: Feeling flat
FRIENDS: Robin
FOES: Gotham City's criminal community
SKILLS: Delivering electric shocks
GEAR: Electro suit

FIRST SET: LEGO DC Universe Super Heroes Batman Visual Dictionary
SET NUMBER: N/A
YEAR: 2012

Light blue lines show where electricity can be generated

BATMAN

BLOWING HOT AND COLD

This minifigure uses the second version of Batman's LEGO cowl

Frosty expression

HEADED FOR HEAT
Batman dons a tan Batsuit for rescuing Robin from Rā's al Ghūl's sandy hideout. His desert fatigues blend in with the arid wasteland—once he gets out of his black Bat Buggy.

White polar Batsuit blends in with the snow

VITAL STATS
LIKES: Keeping his cool
DISLIKES: Being given the cold shoulder
FRIENDS: Aquaman
FOES: Mr. Freeze
SKILLS: Piloting the Batboat
GEAR: Batarang

FIRST SET: Arctic Batman vs. Mr. Freeze: Aquaman on Ice
SET NUMBER: 76000
YEAR: 2013

AVAILABLE IN JUST ONE LEGO® set, Arctic Batman charges to the coldest place on Earth to rescue Aquaman from the chilly clutches of Mr. Freeze. A camouflaged Caped Crusader will soon best the refrigerated rogue.

48

BATMAN

READY FOR ANYTHING

Gas mask protects from Scarecrow's fear gas

Black head piece with lime-green printed visor

CRIMINAL MASTERMINDS are constantly coming up with more outlandish ways to terrorize Gotham City. To keep one step ahead of them, the Dark Knight has equipment for every occasion. This gas mask protects him from Scarecrow's toxic and terrifying fear gas.

VITAL STATS

LIKES: Fresh air
DISLIKES: Toxic gas
FRIENDS: Farmer, Blue Beetle
FOES: Scarecrow, Killer Moth
SKILLS: Filtering air
GEAR: Batcopter, Batarang, gas mask

FIRST SET: Batman: Scarecrow Harvest of Fear
SET NUMBER: 76054
YEAR: 2016

BREATH OF FRESH AIR
A Batarang is no good against poisonous air, but it is effective against Scarecrow's pitchfork. The gas mask buys Batman time to track down the source and teach the villain a lesson.

COSMIC CAPED CRUSADER

VITAL STATS

- **LIKES:** Exploring
- **DISLIKES:** Extraterrestrial thieves
- **FRIENDS:** Green Lantern
- **FOES:** Sinestro
- **SKILLS:** Space flight
- **GEAR:** Extending wings

FIRST SET: Green Lantern vs. Sinestro
SET NUMBER: 76025
YEAR: 2015

Silver cowl with shorter ears

Wings in closed formation

Silver arms and legs

SPACE FLIGHT

The Space Batman variant comes with two translucent plastic capes. Remove Batman's rocket pack to switch over to the outstretched wings and take flight after Sinestro.

IN SPACE, two heads are better than one. The first head of this Cosmic Caped Crusader variant is printed with a special visor and breathing apparatus. It also comes with a separate, standard two-sided head.

BATMAN
HIGH FLYER

VITAL STATS

LIKES: Flying high
DISLIKES: Bumpy landings
FRIENDS: Birds in the sky
FOES: Catwoman
SKILLS: Swooping after jewel thieves
GEAR: Wings, jetpack, Batarang

FIRST SET: Catwoman Catcycle City Chase
SET NUMBER: 6858
YEAR. 2012

Jetpack powers flight

UNLIKE SUPERMAN, Batman can't fly under his own steam. But he does have gadgets to help him patrol the skies and fight crime above the rooftops.

Torso appears in two other sets without the wings

Solid blue wings are a single element that clips around neck

Jetpack outperforms Scarecrow's Gyro-Copter

Double-wing piece

VITAL STATS

LIKES: Aerial attacks
DISLIKES: Gravity
FRIENDS: Crows
FOES: Scarecrow
SKILLS: Chasing down Gyro-Copters
GEAR: Flaming jetpack, wings, Grapple hook

FIRST SET: Scarecrow Fearful Face-off
SET NUMBER: 70913
YEAR: 2017

Transparent flames with adjustable boosters

DEEP-SEA DETECTIVE

Alternative face print has a scuba mask

Harpoon at the ready

Breathing apparatus leading to air tanks worn on the back

TEST DIVE
Even though Black Manta abducting the Boy Wonder is annoying, it does give Batman a chance to test the brand-new Batsub. And he can trial his new scuba face print, too. It's not all bad, then!

NO VILLAIN is safe from Batman—not even on the water. This deep-sea variant is ready to dive straight into the deep end with unique scuba gear printing on his body. It's a good thing his gadgets are all waterproof!

Flippers for fast swimming action

VITAL STATS
LIKES: Diving
DISLIKES: Maritime crime
FRIENDS: Commissioner Gordon
FOES: The Penguin
SKILLS: First-class swimmer
GEAR: Scuba gear, harpoon

FIRST SET: Batman: The Penguin Face Off
SET NUMBER: 76010
YEAR: 2014

BAT ON THE WATER

VITAL STATS

LIKES: Scuba vacations
DISLIKES: Sand in his sandwiches
FRIENDS: Alfred
FOES: The Penguin
SKILLS: Relaxing
GEAR: Flippers, breather

FIRST SET: Batcave Break-in
SET NUMBER: 70909
YEAR: 2017

Scuba suit hangs in Batman's wardrobe

CRIMINALS DON'T stick to the land, so Batman doesn't either. His collection of Batboats and Subs help, but sometimes he just has to get out and sink to the Super-Villains' level.

Spiked flail for self-defense

VITAL STATS

LIKES: Buried treasure
DISLIKES: Walking the plank
FRIENDS: Shipmates
FOES: Sharks
SKILLS: Swashbuckling
GEAR: Cutlass, spiked flail

FIRST SET: LEGO *DC Comics Super Heroes: Character Encyclopedia, first edition*
SET NUMBER: N/A
YEAR: 2016

Scuba mask matches cowl

VITAL STATS

LIKES: Swimming with the fish
DISLIKES: Sleeping with the fish
FRIENDS: Aquaman
FOES: Ocean Master
SKILLS: Battling in his Batsub
GEAR: Batsub, flippers, breather

FIRST SET: Batman Batsub and the Underwater Clash
SET NUMBER: 76116
YEAR: 2019

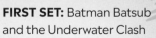

Leather Utility Belt worn as a bandolier

DID YOU KNOW?

This exclusive buccaneering minifigure was available only with the first trade edition of this book.

THE ALIEN KNIGHT

Unique purple cowl

Two-sided face with stubble and growl on one side and smile on the other

VITAL STATS

LIKES: Bright colors
DISLIKES: Shaving
FRIENDS: Batman
FOES: The criminals of Zur-En-Arrh
SKILLS: Hand-to-hand fighting
GEAR: Baseball bat

FIRST SET: Batman of Zur-En-Arrh
SET NUMBER: SDCC036
YEAR: 2014

DID YOU KNOW?

This version of the Caped Crusader first appeared in a 1940 Batman story called *The Superman of Planet X*.

EXTRA-SPECIAL EXTRATERRESTRIAL

The alien Batman's garish colors continue on the minifigure's back. You can also see his yellow Utility Belt complete with pockets and Tiano's radio, capable of scrambling security systems.

Dark purple cape also worn by Bizarro

ALIEN SCIENTIST TIANO spent years monitoring Earth. Impressed by Batman, Tiano became a cowled Caped Crusader for his home planet, Zur-En-Arrh. This colorful minifigure was an exclusive Comic-Con release.

Bat-shaped medallion

VITAL STATS

LIKES: Roller discos
DISLIKES: Falling over
FRIENDS: Tears of Batman
FOES: Bouncers
SKILLS: Gravity-defying spins and jumps
GEAR: Roller skates

FIRST SET: Disco Batman—Tears of Batman
SET NUMBER: 30607
YEAR: 2017

THE MAN IN BLACK—and sometimes gray or blue—has plenty of sparkly secrets in his extensive closet. Work suits can get boring, so he likes to dress up outlandishly in his spare time.

Golden roller skates

VITAL STATS

LIKES: Clowns
DISLIKES: Clown snakes
FRIENDS: Disco Batman
FOES: The Joker
SKILLS: Expressing his emotions
GEAR: None

FIRST SET: Disco Batman—Tears of Batman
SET NUMBER: 30607
YEAR: 2017

First bright-red cowl element

VITAL STATS

LIKES: Discos
DISLIKES: When the music stops
FRIENDS: Disco Robin, Disco Batgirl
FOES: Disco The Joker
SKILLS: Dancing the night away
GEAR: None

FIRST SET: The Joker Manor
SET NUMBER: 70922
YEAR: 2017

Clown-style pom-pom buttons

Shiny gold cape has one white side

Diamante-covered tuxedo

ALL MIXED UP

CREATED BY BIZARRO using his LexCorp duplicator ray, Batzarro is a weird mixed-up version of the Dark Knight and a member of the Bizarro League. While Batman is super-smart, Batzarro is, well, not.

Double-sided head showing Batzarro snarling

Flipped bat-symbol

Cape in tatters

VITAL STATS

LIKES: Committing crimes
DISLIKES: Batman
FRIENDS: Bizarro
FOES: The Justice League
SKILLS: Causing chaos
GEAR: None

FIRST SET: LEGO® DC Comics Super Heroes: Justice League vs. Bizarro League DVD/ Blu-Ray
SET NUMBER: N/A
YEAR: 2015

YELLOW FELLOW
Batman also falls afoul of evil when he becomes Sinestro Batman in a Yellow Lantern costume. The yellow ring doesn't hold power over him for long—but his 2018 minifigure is stuck like this.

DID YOU KNOW?
Batzarro may look scary, but in the end he teams up with the Justice League to defeat Darkseid.

WHEN YOUR DAY JOB is a serious business and your night job is a matter of life and death, it's nice to be a bit silly in your free time.

VITAL STATS

LIKES: Bat-cat mash-ups
DISLIKES: Big game hunters
FRIENDS: Partygoers
FOES: Party poopers
SKILLS: Finding the best parties
GEAR: Batarang, grappling hook, map of Gotham City

FIRST SET: Batman Battle Pod
SET NUMBER: 5004929
YEAR: 2017

Outfit tried on briefly for Jim Gordon's retirement party

VITAL STATS

LIKES: The Highlands
DISLIKES: Pants
FRIENDS: Highlanders
FOES: Shortlanders
SKILLS: Playing the bagpipes
GEAR: Silver sword

FIRST SET: THE LEGO® BATMAN MOVIE: *Chaos in Gotham City*
SET NUMBER: N/A
YEAR: 2017

Tiger-striped tuxedo

Golden torque around neck

Bat-symbol brooch pins his Scottish-style plaid

Traditional Scottish Highland dress

Green plaid kilt

BATMAN
GUARDIAN OF GOTHAM

VITAL STATS

LIKES: Batting for justice
DISLIKES: Injustice
FRIENDS: Alfred
FOES: Selina Kyle, The Penguin, The Riddler
SKILLS: Solving riddles
GEAR: Motorcycle, Batarang

FIRST SET: Batman & Selina Kyle Motorcycle Pursuit
SET NUMBER: 76179
YEAR: 2021

New-style cape doesn't cross over at the neck

DID YOU KNOW?
This Batman minifigure is based on his character from *The Batman* movie, released in 2022.

Bat-symbol design new for 2021

Leg print with kneepads and thigh holster strap

ADVENTURE CALLS
When the glow-in-the-dark LEGO Bat-Signal shines, Batman answers the request for help right off the bat. Jumping onto his motorcycle, he roars away to wherever he is needed.

THE WORLD'S GREATEST Detective isn't easily fazed. Whether Batman's solving crimes with Police Commissioner Gordon, running down The Penguin in his Batmobile, or chasing Selina Kyle on his motorcycle, he's the Bat for the job.

BATCAVE OR BUST

When duty calls, Dick flips up the bust of Shakespeare on Bruce's desk to reveal a hidden button. Pressing it opens up a secret entrance to the Batcave!

Dick models his neat hair after Bruce Wayne's

Sensible red sweater over white shirt

Smart blue pants

VITAL STATS

LIKES: Secretly being Robin
DISLIKES: Writing essays
FRIENDS: Bruce Wayne, Alfred
FOES: Catwoman
SKILLS: Tuba playing, bird calls
GEAR: None

FIRST SET: *Batman* Classic TV Series—Batcave
SET NUMBER: 76052
YEAR: 2016

BEING DICK GRAYSON sure is tough! His legal guardian, Bruce Wayne, makes him study hard when he'd rather be working out in the gym. But when Bruce explains it's all part of being a Boy Wonder, Dick reckons life is not so bad after all.

STARSTRUCK ORPHAN

DICK GRAYSON was born into the circus, trained as an acrobat, orphaned, adopted by a super-suave billionaire, and he's still just a kid! He now gets to live in a massive mansion, and his eyes really boggle when he finds out that his new dad, Bruce Wayne, is Batman.

Glasses are molded to hair piece

Large, vulnerable eyes

Jeans replace previous smart blue pants

VITAL STATS

LIKES: Bruce Wayne
DISLIKES: The orphanage
FRIENDS: Batman
FOES: Catwoman
SKILLS: Acrobatics
GEAR: None

FIRST SET: The Bat-Space Shuttle
SET NUMBER: 70923
YEAR: 2018

DAD HUNTER
Neat, tidy, and dressed to impress, Dick performs at Jim Gordon's retirement party. But really the earnest kid has his spectacled sights on Bruce Wayne—the greatest orphan of all time.

DID YOU KNOW?
Dick Grayson, Robin, and Nightwing's minifigures from THE LEGO BATMAN MOVIE all have googly eyes printed on molded glasses.

ROBIN
THE BOY WONDER

Hair-and-glasses piece used for Dick Grayson now has a green eye print

DID YOU KNOW?

Several people have fought crime as Robin, including Dick Grayson, Jason Todd, Tim Drake, and Damian Wayne.

VITAL STATS

LIKES: Staying up late
DISLIKES: School nights
FRIENDS: Batgirl
FOES: Catwoman
SKILLS: Dodging falling lampposts
GEAR: None

FIRST SET: Catwoman Catcycle Chase
SET NUMBER: 70902
YEAR: 2017

Teeny-tiny green shorts

High red boots

TWINKLE TOES

Acrobatic training is useful for fighting crime but also for disco-tastic dance moves. Robin's flashy movie-based minifigure grooves the night away in The Joker Manor (set 70922).

ON DISCOVERING that his adopted dad is actually Batman, Dick Grayson is quick to embrace the life of a caped crime fighter. Fashioning his own red, green, and yellow outfit from pieces in the Batcave, he creates his own secret identity: Robin.

ROBIN
TRUSTED SIDEKICK

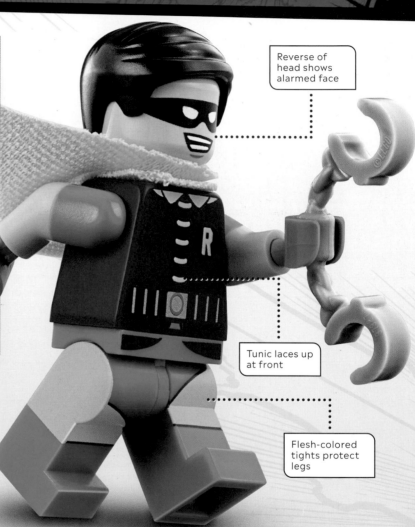

VITAL STATS

LIKES: Riding in the Batmobile
DISLIKES: Not getting to drive the Batmobile
FRIENDS: Batman, Alfred
FOES: Catwoman, The Joker, The Penguin, The Riddler
SKILLS: Honesty, courage
GEAR: Handcuffs

FIRST SET: *Batman* Classic TV Series—Batcave
SET NUMBER: 76052
YEAR: 2016

Reverse of head shows alarmed face

Tunic laces up at front

Flesh-colored tights protect legs

TEEN TITAN

Dick Grayson's Robin helps found the Teen Titans. His 2015 minifigure from Jokerland (set 76035) wears Robin's original insignia, and his sleeves are rolled up ready for hard work. It's not easy being a leader!

THIS COLORFUL SIDEKICK needs an equally colorful oufit. Clad in a smart red tunic and very short green shorts, Dick Grayson's Robin is ready to save the day in style. That's what makes him Batman's best chum and a vital part of the Dynamic Duo!

VITAL STATS

LIKES: Acting alone
DISLIKES: Not being the captain of the ship
FRIENDS: Batman
FOES: Deathstroke
SKILLS: Piloting hover boats
GEAR: Batboat

FIRST SET: Batboat Harbor Pursuit
SET NUMBER: 76034
YEAR: 2015

Longer, shaggier hair for older Robin

New high-tech body armor

DID YOU KNOW?

This minifigure reuses the Robin headpiece from Batman: The Joker Steam Roller (set 76013).

DICK GRAYSON

may be moving on to fight crime as Nightwing, but he still reappears as Robin every now and again. He can't wait for Batman to let him pilot the Batboat for himself, and he wears this darker suit in a fight against Deathstroke.

SUBMARINE SIDEKICK

In 2015, Robin is caught by Black Manta under the sea. His crime-fighting career has never sunk so low, but he is at least dressed for the occasion with flippers, goggles, and a yellow air tank.

Red Robin mask is unique to Jason Todd's minifigure

"R" on chest is a stylized throwing star

More muscly torso

VITAL STATS

LIKES: Scaling new heights
DISLIKES: Being grounded
FRIENDS: Batman
FOES: The Joker
SKILLS: Climbing, acrobatics
GEAR: Grapple hook

FIRST SET: The Joker Batcave Attack
SET NUMBER: 10753
YEAR: 2018

RELIANT ROBIN
A shorter-legged, cartoonish Robin minifigure relies on his Mighty Micros car to get him around on the ground, but he also carries a grapnel, in case there are any walls to climb.

WITH DICK GRAYSON off being Nightwing, Batman is short of a sidekick. He takes new boy Jason Todd under his wing and trains him to take on the mantle of Robin. Todd adopts Robin's identity along with his classic bright primary colors.

ROBIN

TIM DRAKE

WHEN TIM DRAKE realized that Batman needed help, he used his detective skills to figure out the Caped Crusader's secret identity. Batman was so impressed with Tim's abilities that he trained him to become his new sidekick—the third Robin.

Flat hair piece has appeared in LEGO® Pharaoh's Quest and LEGO® City sets

DID YOU KNOW?

Tim Drake is a first-class scientist and engineer and he can use the Batcomputer as well as Batman—maybe even better!

Both 2006 and 2008 Robin minifigure variants wear the same outfit with a bright-yellow cape

VITAL STATS

LIKES: Working things out
DISLIKES: Unsolved puzzles
FRIENDS: Batman, Alfred, Nightwing
FOES: The Penguin, Mr. Freeze
SKILLS: Deduction, swimming
GEAR: Scuba jet

FIRST SET: Robin's Scuba Jet: Attack of The Penguin
SET NUMBER: 7885
YEAR: 2008

ROBIN HOOD

Stepping out on his own, but still fighting crime as Robin, Tim Drake dons a darker, more serious costume. It looks like Tim no longer has time for fun, and certainly this variant does not feature a smiling expression.

DAMIAN WAYNE—THE SON OF BATMAN

VITAL STATS

LIKES: Getting the job done
DISLIKES: The other Robins
FRIENDS: His dad, sometimes
FOES: The Joker, Harley Quinn
SKILLS: Fighting
GEAR: Motorcycle, kendo stick

FIRST SET: Joker's Trike Chase
SET NUMBER: 76159
YEAR: 2020

DID YOU KNOW?

There are four minifigures of Damian Wayne as Robin. As he is a child, they all have short yellow capes and short legs, but only this variant's are posable.

Smirk can be swapped for a more aggressive expression

Torso is a more detailed version of 2014 and 2016 variants

Short, scalloped cape is unique to Damian's Robin

JAILBIRD

A 2016 hooded minifigure of Damian Wayne puts the "son" into "prison" when he's locked up in Rā's al Ghūl's secret headquarters in the desert. Will his dad, in desert fatigues, rescue him?

DAMIAN IS THE SON of Bruce Wayne. Brought up by his assassin mother, Damian is a particularly skilled child. On arriving in Gotham City, he demanded that he take on the role of Robin. Tim Drake reluctantly stood aside.

NIGHTWING

BOY WONDER NO MORE

Mask shaped like wings spread in flight

VITAL STATS

LIKES: Going his own way
DISLIKES: Being told what to do
FRIENDS: Batman
FOES: Poison Ivy
SKILLS: Martial arts
GEAR: 2 escrima sticks

FIRST SET: Nightwing
SET NUMBER: 30606
YEAR: 2016

DICK GRAYSON WAS the first Robin, fighting crime alongside Batman. As he grew older, he wanted to go his own way. He chose Nightwing as his new identity after Superman told him about a legendary Kryptonian character with the same name.

Blue and black costume echoes the wingspan of a bird or a dragon

DID YOU KNOW?

Nightwing's new black-and-red costume first appeared in the DC Comics in 2013.

WINGED WONDER

Just like his mentor, Batman, Nightwing has plenty of cool vehicles at his disposal. His rocket glider allows him to patrol the skies of Gotham City in his new red costume, keeping an eagle eye out for trouble.

NIGHTWING
GOING SOLO

Bat cowl is unique to this minifigure

Clip-on bat wing pieces created for LEGO® Legends of Chima™ theme in 2014

Maybe one day he'll grow into the long cape?

VITAL STATS

LIKES: Tagging along with the Bat Family
DISLIKES: Not having his own look
FRIENDS: Batman, Alfred, Barbara Gordon
FOES: The Joker, Harley Quinn
SKILLS: Acrobatics
GEAR: Wings

FIRST SET: The Joker Manor
SET NUMBER: 70922
YEAR: 2017

NIGHT WHEELS
Older and more streetwise, Nightwing's 2018 minifigure steers his own path. He has little Mighty Micro legs, but he's big on confidence and aggression as he goes after The Joker's chilling ice-cream truck.

THIS NIGHTWING WANTS to be a big Super Hero, but he hasn't found his own way yet. In THE LEGO BATMAN MOVIE, Dick looks like a kid who's raided his dad's wardrobe and come out swamped in an oversized Batsuit.

NIGHTWING

SOLO FLYER

Nightwing's first two-tone winged mask

Previously spiky hair is now longer and shaggier

Turn the head to see an aggressive expression

More detailed torso with blue muscle contours

VITAL STATS

LIKES: Independence
DISLIKES: Other people's rules
FRIENDS: Batman, Batgirl
FOES: Mr. Freeze, Man-Bat, Bronze Tiger
SKILLS: Flying the Batjet
GEAR: Batjet, escrima sticks

FIRST SET: Mobile Bat Base
SET NUMBER: 76160
YEAR: 2020

NIGHT RIDER

Nightwing's first minifigure rides this streamlined cycle to help Batman foil an escape from Arkham Asylum (set 7785). It has space for his two martial arts fighting sticks, also known as escrima.

NIGHTWING HAS MADE a name for himself as an independent crime fighter, but he still teams up with Batman, Batgirl, and the Mobile Bat Base to round up Super-Villains. He gets to pilot the Batjet and put his acrobatic skills to use in the sky.

69

COMMISSIONER GORDON

CHIEF OF GOTHAM CITY POLICE

SWAT'S GOING ON?
Gordon doesn't just sit behind a desk. He gets out in the field in his SWAT (Special Weapons Attack Team) gear. But can a bulletproof vest really protect him from villains like Bane?

Clip stops tie from falling in his coffee

Calm, determined expression in the face of danger

Gotham City police badge

VITAL STATS

LIKES: Law and order
DISLIKES: Crime and deceit
FRIENDS: Batman
FOES: The Riddler
SKILLS: Keeping the peace
GEAR: Police car

FIRST SET: Batwing and The Riddler Heist
SET NUMBER: 76120
YEAR: 2019

UNLIKE MOST OF THE Gotham City police force, James Gordon is an honest cop. While Jim doesn't always approve of Batman's methods, he realizes that the Dark Knight is Gotham City's last hope against dangerous Super-Villains like The Riddler.

Hair piece is worn by a Joker minifigure in lime green

Mustache is beginning to gray

GCPD detectives wear suits rather than police uniforms

MIND MAP

Commissioner Gordon and Batman put their heads together to solve The Riddler's puzzles. The Batcave provides them with high-tech code-breaking computers and a large map of Gotham City.

VITAL STATS

LIKES: Cracking cases
DISLIKES: Safecrackers
FRIENDS: Batman, Alfred, the Drifter
FOES: The Riddler, Selina Kyle
SKILLS: Knowing when to get help from Batman
GEAR: City map

FIRST SET: Batcave: The Riddler Face-off
SET NUMBER: 76183
YEAR: 2021

FIGHTING WRONGDOING in Gotham City doesn't leave James Gordon much time for himself—or to shave. His minifigure's darker suit matches the shadow that has fallen over the city with the latest wave of Super-Villainous crime.

YEARS OF BEING the Gotham City chief of police have taken their toll. Just look at those bags under Jim's eyes, and his hair has gone gray now. Despite dedicating his career to ridding the streets of crime, Super-Villains keep making comebacks.

Crumpled clothes reflect his commitment to the demanding job

WANTED
THE JOKER

The Joker is the bane of Gordon's life

VITAL STATS

LIKES: Clean streets
DISLIKES: Clean getaways
FRIENDS: Honest cops
FOES: Dishonest cops
SKILLS: Putting villains behind bars
GEAR: Flyer, walkie-talkie

FIRST SET: Collectible THE LEGO BATMAN MOVIE Minifigures Series
SET NUMBER: 71017
YEAR: 2017

LAST HURRAH
Honored with medals, a sash, and speeches, Jim Gordon is meant to be celebrating his retirement, but The Joker has other ideas. The former police chief leaps into action—he's not washed up yet!

BARBARA GORDON

NEW POLICE COMMISSIONER

TOP OF HER CLASS at police school, Barbara Gordon follows in the crime-fighting footsteps of her father as Gotham City Police Commissioner. But she's no carbon copy. She has a radical four-point program to shake up policing. And it doesn't revolve around Batman.

VITAL STATS

LIKES: Statistics and accountability
DISLIKES: Vigilantes
FRIENDS: Batman, sometimes
FOES: All the Arkham escapees
SKILLS: Responsible policing
GEAR: Walkie-talkie

FIRST SET: Arkham Asylum
SET NUMBER: 70912
YEAR: 2017

Striped gray and white vest ....

Gotham City police badge proudly worn

THE FRONT LINE

Barbara springs to the defense of Gotham City in her bulletproof GCPD gear. But the by-the-book chief is sure to marry action with actual laws, ethics, and accountability. Paperwork is important, too!

BATGIRL

CHIEF OF POLICE IN DISGUISE

VITAL STATS

LIKES: Teamwork
DISLIKES: Rogue Super Heroes
FRIENDS: Robin
FOES: Catwoman
SKILLS: Stronger, faster, and smarter than Batman
GEAR: 2 Batarangs

FIRST SET: Catwoman Catcycle Chase
SET NUMBER: 70902
YEAR: 2017

Ponytail clips onto cowl

DID YOU KNOW?

Vacation Batgirl—a variant of this minifigure with a wetsuit and surfboard—made a splash in the 2018 Collectible Minifigures series.

Yellow Batarangs are unique to Batgirl

Dual-molded legs have straps printed on the side

LOOSE CANNON

Villains are flying at Batgirl like cannonballs! Can she banish them to the Phantom Zone with her large red projector? More importantly, once there, will they behave?

NEW POLICE COMMISSIONER Barbara Gordon doesn't want vigilantes operating solo in her city. She believes in policing *inside* the law. But if you can't beat them, join them. Barbara becomes Batgirl—and is often one step ahead of Batman.

BATGIRL

THE COMMISSIONER'S DAUGHTER

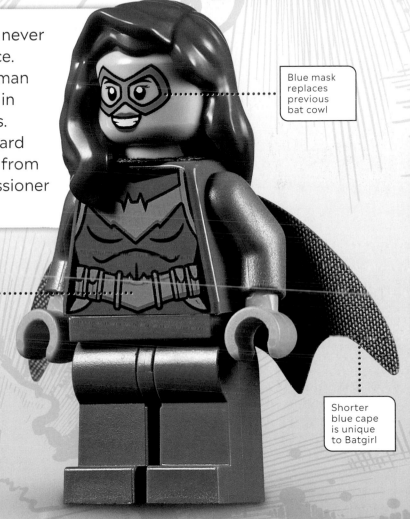

THIS BARBARA GORDON never made it into the police force. She had always been a Batman fan, and she soon followed in the Dark Knight's footsteps. However, she has to work hard to keep her identity secret from her detective dad, Commissioner Jim Gordon.

Blue mask replaces previous bat cowl

Utility Belt has bat-shaped clasp

Shorter blue cape is unique to Batgirl

VITAL STATS

LIKES: Being part of a team
DISLIKES: Being ignored
FRIENDS: Batman, Nightwing
FOES: Man-Bat, Mr. Freeze, Bronze Tiger
SKILLS: Acrobatic tricks
GEAR: Batquad

FIRST SET: Mobile Bat Base
SET NUMBER: 76160
YEAR: 2020

GIRL POWER
Batgirl's 2014 variant has a purple cape and long hair flowing from her Batman-inspired cowl. At first, Batman wasn't sure about her, but she soon proved her worth fighting villains—from The Joker's henchman to the Clown Prince of Crime himself.

BATMAN'S COUSIN

BEING A VIGILANTE runs in Batman's family. His cousin Kate Kane takes up a crusading cape after training in the military. Batman inspires her to be Batwoman, but he doesn't always approve of her more ruthless tactics.

White head piece has plain white goggles under cowl

Mask molded to hair piece

More elegant bat-symbol in scarlet

Fully stocked Utility Belt

High-tech suit designed by Kate Kane's father

VITAL STATS

LIKES: Protecting the innocent
DISLIKES: Rules
FRIENDS: Batman
FOES: OMAC
SKILLS: Martial arts, military training
GEAR: Batjet, Batarang

FIRST SET: Batman: Brother Eye Takedown
SET NUMBER: 76111
YEAR: 2018

WINGING IT

Every bat needs wings, even Batwoman. She swoops into action in the Batjet with her eyes on the prize: taking down the Brother Eye satellite that is controling its OMAC army.

VITAL STATS

NAME: Bat-Mite
LIKES: Mischief
DISLIKES: Not being appreciated
FRIENDS: The Bat Family
FOES: Crooks
SKILLS: Reality warping
GEAR: Comic book tile *Detective Comics #27* (Batman's first appearance)

FIRST SET: Collectible LEGO DC Super Heroes Minifigures Series
SET NUMBER: 71026
YEAR: 2020

Cartoonish toothy grin

Magical imp has short legs

Supergirl's hair piece from 2015

VITAL STATS

NAME: Vicki Vale
LIKES: Hunting down the truth
DISLIKES: Fake news
FRIENDS: Batman
FOES: The Joker
SKILLS: Reporting the news
GEAR: Camera

FIRST SET: 1989 Batmobile
SET NUMBER: 76139
YEAR: 2019

Torso is also worn by an unnamed wizard in the LEGO® Harry Potter™ theme

Mask hides the identity of Jaime Reyes

VITAL STATS

NAME: Blue Beetle
LIKES: Teen Titans
DISLIKES: Bug spray
FRIENDS: Batman
FOES: Scarecrow, Killer Moth
SKILLS: Flight, creating weapons and defenses
GEAR: Power element, wings

FIRST SET: Batman: Scarecrow Harvest of Fear
SET NUMBER: 76054
YEAR: 2016

Dual-molded legs have blue boots

FRIENDSHIPS can be complicated. Bat-Mite has a knack for havoc rather than help, but Blue Beetle is a promising rookie. And will journalist Vicki Vale keep Batman's secret?

BEHIND ME? I'M NOT FALLING FOR THAT!

WHAT'S A CROOK TO DO when there are Super Heroes at every turn? Come up with ever crazier and more outlandish plots, that's what! Gotham City is riddled with fearsome felons who are up to no good. Criminal kingpins call the shots and heinous henchmen help out.

THE JOKER
THE CLOWN PRINCE OF CRIME

THIS CLOWNISH character is no fool—he's the prince of crime in Gotham City! His grin hides a hatred of Batman and Robin, and his jokes always have a sting in the tail.

VITAL STATS

LIKES: A good laugh
DISLIKES: The Batwing on his tail
FRIENDS: Henchman
FOES: Batman
SKILLS: Flying his Joker Copter
GEAR: Joker Copter, Joker card, "Bang" weapon

FIRST SET: The Batwing: The Joker's Aerial Assault
SET NUMBER: 7782
YEAR: 2006

Hair piece with pointed corners was created in black in 2002 for a vampire

Don't sniff the flower—it spits acid!

VITAL STATS

LIKES: Blowing stuff up
DISLIKES: Brushing his teeth
FRIENDS: Mechanics
FOES: Batman, Robin
SKILLS: Driving his hotrod
GEAR: Hotrod, dynamite, giant mallet

FIRST SET: The Joker Batcave Attack
SET NUMBER: 10753
YEAR: 2018

Double-sided head has yellow-toothed grin and a smirk

Lurid torso with lime-green bow tie and blue vest is worn by four variants

VITAL STATS

LIKES: Frozen treats
DISLIKES: Antidotes for toxic gas
FRIENDS: His goons
FOES: Nightwing
SKILLS: Selling toxic ice-cream
GEAR: Ice-cream truck, popsicle

FIRST SET: Mighty Micros: Nightwing vs. The Joker
SET NUMBER: 76093
YEAR: 2018

Lopsided evil grin

Short, nonposable legs

THE JOKER
GIGGLING GANGSTER

VITAL STATS

LIKES: Looking good
DISLIKES: Being scruffy
FRIENDS: His loyal goons
FOES: Batman
SKILLS: Causing devastation

FIRST SET: 1989 Batmobile
SET NUMBER: 76139
YEAR: 2019

LEGO® fedora rarely seen in this color

A CRIMINAL MASTERMIND can still take care of his appearance. This outrageous outfit betrays The Joker's gangster roots, adding a little sinister style to the proceedings. And of course, he's still smiling.

Long purple tailcoat

Plaid trousers

MONSTER MOTORS

It was no laughing matter when The Joker's 2014 Steam Roller carved a crazy path through Gotham City. But The Joker's popgun couldn't save him from the combined might of Batman, Robin, and Batgirl.

DID YOU KNOW?

The designs of these two 2019 and 2014 minifigures are inspired by the 1989 *Batman* movie.

81

THE JOKER
THE DARK KNIGHT'S DARKEST VILLAIN

VITAL STATS

LIKES: Makeup
DISLIKES: Revealing his real face
FRIENDS: His goons
FOES: Batman
SKILLS: Causing chaos
GEAR: Just a winning smile

FIRST SET: The Tumbler
SET NUMBER: 76023
YEAR: 2014

DID YOU KNOW?
This minifigure is based on The Joker's appearance in the 2008 *The Dark Knight* movie.

Wide grin flashes yellow teeth

The Joker's face, hair, torso, and legs are all exclusive to this one set

The Joker's torso displays four layers of clothing: a checkered shirt, two vests, and a purple overcoat!

Wallet chain

WILD SIDE
The alternate faces on this exclusive minifigure show two equally scary expressions. Added to this, The Joker's wild, scruffy hair is a far cry from his usual styled locks and the dark eye makeup further adds to a sinister first impression.

THIS MINIFIGURE OF The Joker has a natural skin tone smothered in chalk-white makeup and a painted-on smile. But there's nothing funny about his terrible crimes. The Joker has never been so unpredictable. Batman had better watch out!

STILL MAD, BAD,

and dangerous to know, The Joker is up to his peculiar tricks. He's taken his chalk-white makeup to extremes, dressing up in full mime costume. Only his puckered red lips add color to his look.

Laughter lines around the eyes from too much laughing

Black-and-white version of The Joker's outfit from 1989 Batmobile (set 76139)

DID YOU KNOW?

These two characters are based on scenes from the 1989 *Batman* movie.

Fabric tails for coat

White spats over black shoes

HIT PARADE

Lawrence is a henchman tasked with carrying The Joker's boombox. There's no doubt about the goon's loyalty—he has The Joker playing cards on his arm and a portrait of The Joker on his chest.

VITAL STATS

LIKES: His gang of miming goons
DISLIKES: Glass boxes
FRIENDS: Lawrence "The Boombox" Goon
FOES: Batman
SKILLS: Getting his message across
GEAR: Sharpened quill

FIRST SET: 1989 Batwing
SET NUMBER: 76161
YEAR: 2020

WITH HIS GROTESQUE grin, lurid green hair, and bright-pink suit, The Joker is never going to make it as a sneak thief! Instead, he likes to live large as he launches plots to steal paintings, build a flying saucer, and beat Batman at a surfing contest.

The Joker's lighter green hair piece is unique to these two variants

Three-piece suit is packed with pranks

DID YOU KNOW?

These two minifigures are styled on The Joker from the classic *Batman* TV show, played by Cesar Romero. He refused to shave his mustache, so it was covered with makeup.

VITAL STATS

LIKES: Laughing
DISLIKES: Being laughed at
FRIENDS: Lab assistants
FOES: Batman
SKILLS: Magic tricks and inventing gadgets
GEAR: Grappling hook

FIRST SET: *Batman* Classic TV Series Batmobile
SET NUMBER: 76188
YEAR: 2021

LAB GRAB

When The Joker gets his hands on Batman's lab, who knows what chemical concoctions he will cook up! Going by the grin on his 2016 minifigure, it might be a batch of laughing gas.

84

THE JOKER'S MANIC GRIN is back and bigger than ever in THE LEGO® BATMAN MOVIE. He's out to cause chaos at every turn, but he ends up helping save Gotham City because, well, if he's not Batman's Greatest Enemy, then who is he?

VITAL STATS

LIKES: Playing with Batman
DISLIKES: Being ignored by Batman
FRIENDS: All escaped prisoners
FOES: Batman
SKILLS: Floating away
GEAR: Balloon backpack

FIRST SET: The Joker Balloon Escape
SET NUMBER: 70900
YEAR: 2017

Ten variants of The Joker share this more bouffant green hair piece

Alternate face has an oversized laughing mouth

Neck brace for attaching backpack

Coat tails are twice as long as his body

FIRING ON ALL CYLINDERS

With new short, yellow sleeves, The Joker sinks to new lows in his bouncing Notorious Lowrider. His popgun fires a flag with "BANG" on it, and his car's trunk pops open to fire hidden shooters.

THE JOKER

ARKHAM INMATE

Same hair as other versions of The Joker from THE LEGO BATMAN MOVIE

Double-sided face also has huge laughing mouth

Bright-orange jumpsuit says "ARKHAM" on the back

PARTNERS IN CRIME

The doctors at Arkham Asylum hoped they could prepare The Joker for civilized law-abiding society, but the only thing the 2013 Super-Villain prepared behind bars was further crimes—particularly with a certain Dr. Harleen Quinzel!

DID YOU KNOW?

Four Joker minifigures have been sentenced to wearing orange prison jumpsuits. The back of the 2013 version is printed with his inmate number—109370.

VITAL STATS

LIKES: Freedom
DISLIKES: Being brought to justice
FRIENDS: The Arkham Asylum inmates
FOES: Batman, Barbara Gordon, GCPD officers
SKILLS: Escapology
GEAR: Handcuffs

FIRST SET: Arkham Asylum
SET NUMBER: 70912
YEAR: 2017

ARKHAM ASYLUM high-security prison is The Joker's home away from home, although he never stays for long. Batman thought he had the Clown Prince of Crime under lock and key, until the dastardly villain schemed his way out.

THE JOKER
STILL THINKS HE'S FUNNY

VITAL STATS

LIKES: Poisoning food
DISLIKES: Food that stains
FRIENDS: Sweet villains
FOES: Health inspectors
SKILLS: Cooking with (laughing) gas
GEAR: Joker card, cotton candy

FIRST SET: Collectible LEGO® DC Super Heroes Minifigures Series
SET NUMBER: 71026
YEAR: 2020

Color and style of this hair piece is new for The Joker

The top of the cotton candy is a pink minifigure head element

DID YOU KNOW?

The white-suited Joker minifigure with cotton candy is based on his character from *The Dark Knight Returns*.

BEWARE JOKERS offering sweet treats. The archcriminal started out with a tasteless plan to sell toxic gas ice-creams, but now he's moved on to poisoned cotton candy. His pure white suit is no sign of innocence.

CLOWN PRINCE OF PARTIES

The Disco Joker isn't interested in poisoning anyone right now. He's taken over Wayne Manor and unleashed a diabolical funfair. He's just enjoying the chaos—and the disco music.

NO CLOWNING AROUND

VITAL STATS

LIKES: Being a grump
DISLIKES: Smiling
FRIENDS: The Joker
FOES: Batman
SKILLS: Helicopter pilot
GEAR: Laughing gas bomb

FIRST SET: Batwing Battle Over Gotham City
SET NUMBER: 6863
YEAR: 2012

This henchman never fancies turning his frown upside down

Lime-green to match The Joker's vest

Black gloves leave no fingerprints

BACK TO BASICS

There's no mistaking who this moaning minifigure works for. Not only are his clothes The Joker's trademark colors, but also the Clown Prince of Crime's face is emblazoned on his back.

THE JOKER'S HENCHMAN likes to crack safes but not smiles. This grouch is never happy. Maybe he doesn't like having his face painted. He'd better watch out, just in case The Joker gives him a dose of all that laughing gas!

THE GRUMPY GOON

VITAL STATS

LIKES: Destruction
DISLIKES: Organized fun
FRIENDS: The Joker
FOES: Batman, Robin, Batgirl
SKILLS: Deconstruction
GEAR: Crowbar

FIRST SET: Batman: The Joker Steamroller
SET NUMBER: 76013
YEAR: 2014

Hard hat for falling debris

Angry face shows through splotchy clown makeup

Orange construction vest is new and exclusive for this variant of The Joker's goon

Tool of destruction

A JOKER ORIGINAL

A quick glance at the henchman's back shows that The Joker has been busy customizing his goon's bright-orange wardrobe. The fiend enjoys a play on words.

THE JOKER'S RIGHT-HAND goon still hasn't cheered up. You would think that the miserable minifigure could at least manage a smirk. After all, he's been given free rein by his boss to demolish Gotham City. Some people are never happy.

CATWOMAN

PURRING PLUNDERER

CATWOMAN WOULD like Batman if it wasn't for all his do-gooding! Instead, she sets her cat's eyes on ridding Gotham City of its Dynamic Duo and risking her nine lives on feline felonies such as sneaking into Wayne Manor!

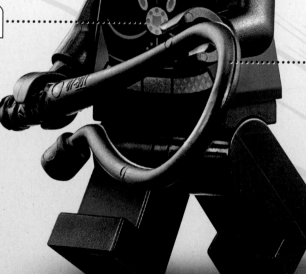

Cat ears attached to headband

Catty look can be swapped for a merrier, masked face

Gold medallion worn over catsuit

LEGO whip element also used as backpack cables for Mr. Freeze, Firefly, and Condiment King

VITAL STATS

LIKES: Long stretches
DISLIKES: Long stretches in jail
FRIENDS: The Joker, The Penguin, The Riddler
FOES: Batman and Robin
SKILLS: Cat burglary
GEAR: Whip

FIRST SET: *Batman Classic TV Series—Batcave*
SET NUMBER: 76052
YEAR: 2016

THE CAT CAME BACK

Catwoman knows all about Wayne Manor after posing as Dick Grayson's dance teacher. She's not scared of falling off its high walls, because a cat always lands on its feet!

SUPERSTITIONS VARY as to whether a black cat crossing your path is lucky or unlucky. But one thing is for sure: Catwoman can only mean trouble. Especially if you have jewels you would rather hang on to.

Turn the head to swap eyes for printed white goggles

First Catwoman minifigure gives a hint of future purple costumes

VITAL STATS

LIKES: High-speed chases
DISLIKES: Justice
FRIENDS: Fellow thieves
FOES: Batman
SKILLS: Robbing and running
GEAR: Motorcycle, whip

FIRST SET: The Batman Dragster: Catwoman Pursuit
SET NUMBER: 7779
YEAR: 2006

VITAL STATS

LIKES: Breaking and entering
DISLIKES: Burglar alarms
FRIENDS: Two-Face, Clayface
FOES: Batman, Robin, Batwoman
SKILLS: Leaving no trace
GEAR: Whip, diamond

FIRST SET: Batcave Clayface Invasion
SET NUMBER: 76122
YEAR: 2019

New red lenses are printed on head piece

Belt with cat's-head clasp

All-black costume for hiding in the shadows

Fitted catsuit for gymnastic tumbling

VITAL STATS

LIKES: Jewels
DISLIKES: Dogs
FRIENDS: Diamonds
FOES: Batman
SKILLS: Cat burglary
GEAR: Mighty Micros car, milk carton

FIRST SET: Mighty Micros: Batman vs. Catwoman
SET NUMBER: 76061
YEAR: 2016

CATWOMAN

GOTHAM CITY'S NUMBER-ONE CAT BURGLAR

VITAL STATS

LIKES: Diamonds
DISLIKES: Getting caught
FRIENDS: Arkham Asylum inmates
FOES: Batman, Batgirl, Robin
SKILLS: Quick getaways
GEAR: Catcycle, whip, red jewel

FIRST SET: Catwoman Catcycle Chase
SET NUMBER: 70902
YEAR: 2017

Mask doubles as a Catcycle helmet

Detachable Utility Belt

New purr-ple catsuit

SOUR PUSS

For once, this cat doesn't land on her feet when the law catches up with her in Arkham Asylum (set 70912). The cat used to getting the cream now has to eat prison slop.

JEWEL THIEF SELINA KYLE has a weakness for glittering diamonds. No gem is safe while Catwoman is on the prowl. A talented gymnast, Selina often has to make acrobatic escapes from Batman.

SELINA KYLE IS definitely a cat person. Since becoming Catwoman, she has dropped the pointy ears and furry tail, but not her love of stealing. She's still the cat's whiskers at burglarizing places of their glittery jewels and is a fur-midable felon.

Double-sided head has a smile or a thoughtful expression

VITAL STATS

LIKES: As many carats as possible
DISLIKES: Costume jewelry
FRIENDS: Batman
FOES: Batman
SKILLS: Unearthing hidden gems
GEAR: Motorcycle, chain, ruby

FIRST SET: Batman & Selina Kyle Motorcycle Pursuit
SET NUMBER: 76179
YEAR: 2021

Cat gloves have sharp claws for silently cutting through glass

Form-fitting catsuit doesn't restrict acrobatic moves and martial arts

WILD CAT CHASE
Selina's motorcycle purrs as she makes her escape from the scene of the crime. The trunk is hiding a precious gem, but Batman is on her tail. Can she get away before he catches her?

THE PENGUIN
ANTARCTIC ADVERSARY

HIGH AND DRY
When The Penguin sticks his beak into the Batcave he floats in on his trademark umbrella, which can also shoot knockout gas, cut glass, self-destruct—and even keep the rain off!

The Penguin thinks that a top hat makes him look taller

The Penguin's black jacket sits over his stripy vest

White gloves cover hands

VITAL STATS

LIKES: Fish and all birds except robins
DISLIKES: Mammals, especially bats
FRIENDS: Catwoman, The Joker, The Riddler
FOES: Batman and Robin
SKILLS: Squawking, scheming
GEAR: Umbrella

FIRST SET: *Batman Classic TV Series—Batcave*
SET NUMBER: 76052
YEAR: 2016

FOES DON'T COME fishier than this feather-ruffling ruffian! Waddling his way through the murky waters of Gotham City's underworld, this version of The Penguin is sporting a lilac-colored top hat and a bow tie.

THE PENGUIN
WRAPPED UP WARM FOR WINTER

VITAL STATS

LIKES: Ice and snow
DISLIKES: Heat
FRIENDS: Robot penguins
FOES: Batman
SKILLS: Cryogenics
GEAR: Duck boat, umbrella

FIRST SET: Batman:
The Penguin Face Off
SET NUMBER: 76010
YEAR: 2014

This variant still wears his monocle

2014 umbrella has a brown handle

Fur edging perfect for chilly crimes

GANGSTER KINGPIN
With a penguin suit, matching purple pants and bow tie, umbrella, and fish, the 2013 Penguin minifigure rules the roost in Batman: Arkham Asylum Breakout (set 10937) and Jokerland (set 76035).

GIGGLING GANGSTER Oswald Cobblepot loves waddling off with other people's riches. The fowl fiend is no featherbrain, although he keeps his secrets safely under his top hat, and is never far from one of his gadget-laden umbrellas.

THE PENGUIN

FREE AS A BIRD

VITAL STATS

LIKES: Sharp tailoring
DISLIKES: Prison jumpsuits
FRIENDS: Sea life
FOES: Batman
SKILLS: Ruffling feathers
GEAR: Duck boat, furled umbrella

FIRST SET: Batboat The Penguin Pursuit!
SET NUMBER: 76158
YEAR: 2020

DRESSED TO IMPRESS

Always impeccably dressed, The Penguin likes to look his best. The original 2006 Penguin minifigure wore an orange vest and is the only one to not have an eye showing through his monocle.

White gloves

Flashiest vest yet

Short purple leg piece was created specially for The Penguin in 2013

DID YOU KNOW?

The Penguin waddled into his first comic book in 1941 in *Detective Comics* #58.

THE PENGUIN HAS smaller than average legs, but he makes up for it with one of the biggest egos in Gotham City. His short LEGO leg piece has no hinges so he can only waddle, but this doesn't hold him back from his dastardly plans.

THE PENGUIN
DAPPER FLAPPER

New tapered top hat

First Penguin minifigure to have a detachable fur collar

VITAL STATS

LIKES: Cruising in his roller
DISLIKES: Traffic wardens
FRIENDS: Arkham Asylum prisoners
FOES: Batman
SKILLS: Snarling
GEAR: Arctic roller, mini escape pod, furled umbrella

FIRST SET: The Penguin Arctic Roller
SET NUMBER: 70911
YEAR: 2017

JAILBIRD

Unlike many of his fellow villains, The Penguin dodged wearing a prison jumpsuit in LEGO® set releases. But his luck ran out with this exclusive figure for THE LEGO BATMAN MOVIE: *The Essential Collection* books.

Polka dots brighten subdued suit

BATMAN'S OLDEST FOE, The Penguin fancies himself as an upstanding Gotham City citizen, but he is not a good egg. Another Penguin minifigure, identical to this one, save for a manically grinning face, is up to fowl play in Batcave Break-in (set 70909).

THE PENGUIN
FALLING FOWL OF THE LAW

Double-sided head has a scheming smile and a fierce scowl

First hair piece for a minifigure of The Penguin

THE PINSTRIPED kingpin of crime has gone up in the world—for the first time, The Penguin has full-size minifigure legs! He has lost his waddle, top hat, and monocle, but his newfound stature and streamlined look show that this villain means business.

VITAL STATS

LIKES: Slicked-back hair
DISLIKES: Ruffled feathers
FRIENDS: Hench-penguins
FOES: Batman
SKILLS: Taking care of business
GEAR: Rocket launcher

FIRST SET: Batmobile: The Penguin Chase
SET NUMBER: 76181
YEAR: 2021

Purple touches hint to his previous costumes

BAT VERSUS BIRD
Batman tracks down The Penguin in his 2021 Batmobile that's turbo-charged with blue flames. Can the battle-ready Batmobile beat the bird's handheld rocket launcher?

Flexible fitted bodysuit allows for acrobatic moves

Emotionless face is based on a mime artist's mask

Removable finger blades

VITAL STATS

LIKES: Synchronization
DISLIKES: Independent thought
FRIENDS: Man-Bat
FOES: Batman, Robin
SKILLS: Martial arts, scratching, and slicing
GEAR: 2 sets of claws

FIRST SET: The Batmobile
SET NUMBER: 70905
YEAR: 2017

DOUBLE WHAMMY
Two identical Kabuki minifigures attack the Batmobile in tandem. The silent and mysterious twins double down on Batman and Robin on the orders of The Penguin.

THEY SAY TWO HEADS are better than one, and two sets of claws are even better. Two of these Kabuki evil twins serve The Penguin as bodyguards. Their look is based on Kabuki—a classical Japanese style of drama and dance.

THE RIDDLER
CRIME IN THE FAST LANE

New stylish hat matches Riddler's impish expression

Hair piece is attached to bowler hat

Question marks continue over the arms and back

VITAL STATS

LIKES: Running Batman down in his racer
DISLIKES: Running out of gas
FRIENDS: Kite Man, Magpie, Calendar Man
FOES: Batman
SKILLS: Firing weapons from a speeding car
GEAR: Question-mark cane, Riddler Racer

FIRST SET: The Riddler Riddle Racer
SET NUMBER: 70903
YEAR: 2017

FASHION VICTIM
Locked up in Arkham Asylum (set 70912), The Riddler loses the right to stylish clothes. No more natty suits for him—prison orange is the new green.

UNQUESTIONABLY, The Riddler is one snappy dresser. In 2017, he dons a full three-piece suit for stealing loot and driving his Riddler Racer. The peculiar Super-Villain is committed to his color scheme; his green-and-purple theme is punctuated only by a crisp white shirt.

THE RIDDLER

AN ENIGMA

Only this version of The Riddler has printed hair

Existing bowler hat shape is now lime

DID YOU KNOW?

The Riddler appears in all three of the LEGO® Batman™ video games, along with his trademark question-mark cane.

RIDDLE ME THIS

In his classic costume, with matching silk cummerbund, mask, and gloves, The Riddler is out to blow the roof off Wayne Manor.

Lime suit is a first for The Riddler

VITAL STATS

LIKES: Quizzes and conundrums
DISLIKES: Easy answers
FRIENDS: The Joker, The Penguin
FOES: Batman, Commissioner Gordon
SKILLS: Robbing banks, chemistry
GEAR: Question-mark cane, dynamite, helicopter

WHEN DOES a question mark mean danger? When it's printed on The Riddler's outfit! This puzzling pest always leaves clues to his quizzical crimes, luring Batman and Robin into baffling booby traps that seem to have no answer.

FIRST SET: Batwing and The Riddler Heist
SET NUMBER: 76120
YEAR: 2019

101

VITAL STATS

LIKES: Anything green
DISLIKES: Red lights
FRIENDS: Scarecrow, Poison Ivy
FOES: Batman, The Flash
SKILLS: Racing dragsters
GEAR: Question-mark cane, money, dragster

FIRST SET: Batman: The Riddler Chase
SET NUMBER: 76012
YEAR: 2014

Gray bowler hat from 2012 variant is now green

Exclusive green jacket with question-mark motif

Purple driving gloves

Two-tone green on legs and arms

ONE OF GOTHAM

City's most confusing villains, Edward Nygma likes to leave a trail of cryptic clues behind to help Batman foil his crimes. No one knows why. It's a mystery, and the most puzzling of all The Riddler's riddles.

CARRIED AWAY

In 2006, The Riddler was carted off to Arkham Asylum (set 7785) sporting a shock of black hair and a simpler green outfit. In 2012, he gained more muscles, more question marks, and a gray bowler hat.

Glasses worn over full face mask

Olive green is a new shade for The Riddler minifigures

Previous question-mark motif reduced to single sewn-on badge

VITAL STATS

LIKES: Taunting Batman with clues
DISLIKES: Batman's answers
FRIENDS: Selina Kyle
FOES: Batman, the Drifter, Alfred, Commissioner Gordon
SKILLS: Creating criminal conundrums
GEAR: Rocket launcher

FIRST SET: Batcave: The Riddler Face-off
SET NUMBER: 76183
YEAR: 2021

DID YOU KNOW?

The clue to this minifigure's appearance is in the 2022 film *The Batman*.

UNDER LOCK AND KEY

The question is, why did The Riddler leave three coded LEGO messages when Batman had the magnifying glass for deciphering them? His minifigure now has plenty of time in the Batcave prison to ponder this puzzle.

HATS OFF TO THE RIDDLER'S ambitions. He's back and more cunning than ever. For the first time, his minifigure reveals a full head of hair, though his face is concealed. Less hidden are his crimes, which he flaunts.

HARLEY QUINN

LAUGHTER IS THE BEST MEDICINE

NO ONE KNEW that The Joker had secretly persuaded prison psychiatrist Harleen Quinzel to become the villainous Harley Quinn. The double-crossing doctor was then on hand to help her puddin' to escape—along with the rest of the inmates, too!

Neat, professional hairstyle

Red scarf is a hint to her other identity

Doctor's name badge

VITAL STATS

LIKES: Gag weapons
DISLIKES: Unrequited love
FRIENDS: The Joker, Poison Ivy
FOES: Batman and Robin
SKILLS: Escapology
GEAR: Computer, syringes, clipboard

FIRST SET: Arkham Asylum
SET NUMBER: 70912
YEAR: 2017

DID YOU KNOW?

Harley Quinn first appeared in a 1992 episode of *Batman: The Animated Series*.

MANIC MAKEUP!

Dr. Quinzel's 2013 minifigure has an office at Arkham with a hidden dressing table. It has all she needs for a quick costume change, plus a poster signed by The Joker!

HARLEY QUINN

DEADLY JESTER

VITAL STATS

LIKES: Roller coasters
DISLIKES: Heroic characters
FRIENDS: The Joker, The Riddler
FOES: Batman, Robin
SKILLS: Setting traps
GEAR: Roller-coaster car

FIRST SET: The Dynamic Duo Funhouse Escape
SET NUMBER: 6857
YEAR: 2012

Harley Quinn was the first minifigure to wear a jester's hat

A revolving head reveals a mischievous grin

Red-and-black card game-inspired design

ARMED TO THE TEETH
The 2008 Harley Quinn (from set 7886) has a wide, manic grin, and her teeth are colored yellow. Perhaps she's smiling so much because she's got her hands on not one but two weapons!

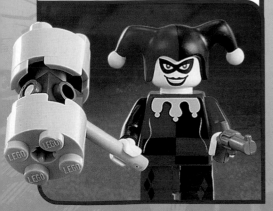

HARLEEN QUINZEL was The Joker's doctor at Arkham Asylum, but instead of curing her criminal patient, she joined him on a crazy crime spree as Harley Quinn. Now, she has fun causing chaos in Gotham City with her beloved puddin', Mr. J!

HARLEY QUINN

TRICOLOR TRICKSTER

Rare red-and-blue hair piece is shared with Harley's Mighty Micros minifigure

Corset design continues on the back

Brutal belt of bullets

VITAL STATS

LIKES: Hair dye
DISLIKES: Being serious
FRIENDS: Deadshot
FOES: Batman
SKILLS: Going flat out on her cycle
GEAR: Bike with hammer attachment

FIRST SET: Gotham City Cycle Chase
SET NUMBER: 76053
YEAR: 2016

HAMMER SLAMMER
Harley likes to smash speed records in her Mighty Micros "wind up" car. In fact, she likes to smash everything! She wields her massive mallet and is ready to whack anyone overtaking in the next lane. Batman had better watch out!

HARLEY LOOKS a little blue in her latest outfit, but her evil grin suggests that she's still happy being bad. Her usual jester's hat has been replaced by a pair of mismatched pigtails, and her belt is bulked out with a row of bullets!

106

New hair piece with corkscrewed pigtails

HARLEY QUINN'S NEW hair piece is as twisted as her personality has become under the influence of The Joker. The clown princess of crime has an updated circus-inspired outfit with her trademark jester colors and patterns.

Diamond design based on playing cards

Unique tutu piece fits between torso and leg elements

VITAL STATS

LIKES: Battling Batwings
DISLIKES: Running out of cannonballs
FRIENDS: The Joker, Poison Ivy, The Penguin
FOES: Batman, Robin
SKILLS: Creating chaos, acrobatics
GEAR: Spinning hammer, mobile cannon

FIRST SET: The Batwing
SET NUMBER: 70916
YEAR: 2017

HIGH-WIRE HAVOC
In her 2015 acrobat suit and jester's hat, Harley rides her "Wheels of Fire" motorcycle down the high wire. She is enjoying the ride a lot more than the upside-down Robin stuck underneath. She likes to keep him hanging.

DIAMOND DEVIANT

VITAL STATS
....

LIKES: Following The Joker
DISLIKES: Batman getting in the way
FRIENDS: The Joker
FOES: Batman, Robin
SKILLS: Making mischievous mayhem
GEAR: Giant hammer

FIRST SET: Joker's Trike Chase
SET NUMBER: 76159
YEAR: 2020

Unique dip-dyed hair piece

Bright-blue-and-pink hair matches her new hammer

Reverse of jacket says "Harley"

CHAIN REACTION
Once an employee of Arkham Asylum, Harley is now an inmate—but not for long. Grinning with glee in her prison jumpsuit, she pulls down a panel of the prison with her motorcycle.

HARLEY'S SIGNATURE red-and-black style is back with a new outfit, but she has all-new hair and makeup. She still loves a laugh, though, and uses her oversize weapon to hammer home any punch line.

THE SCARECROW

MASTER OF FEAR

VITAL STATS

LIKES: Striking fear into the hearts of everyone
DISLIKES: Bullies
FRIENDS: The Arkham Asylum inmates
FOES: Batman and Robin
SKILLS: Escape bids
GEAR: None

FIRST SET: Batman: Arkham Asylum Breakout
SET NUMBER: 10937
YEAR: 2013

Wide-brimmed scarecrow hat

Scary cloth face

Rope fashion accessories

His tattered clothing is also printed on the back of the minifigure

LIVING NIGHTMARE

Luckily, Scarecrow doesn't have nyctophobia (fear of the dark) or cleithrophobia (fear of being locked up) as he spends a lot of time in jail. Not that it would matter, as his earlier 2006 minifigure, in set 7786, had a glow-in-the-dark head!

SHUNNED BY HIS friends and family, phobia expert Dr. Jonathan Crane decided to terrify everyone in Gotham City. As the Scarecrow, he uses his homemade fear gas to bring his victims' worst nightmares to life.

THE SCARECROW

MAN OF STRAW

FEAR THE WORST!

Scarecrow is taking to the sky in his hodgepodge Gyro-Copter to disperse his fear gas bombs far and wide. The flying villain plays on your deepest fears and has spreading terror all stitched up.

2016 molded hair-and-hat piece has new coloring

New face print has chilling smile

Opening of head sack makes a frilled collar

CREAM OF THE CROP

Dressed in orangey-brown cast-offs, the 2016 Scarecrow is harvesting more than crops. His harvester has sharp rotating blades and a tank of fear gas with room for captured minifigures.

VITAL STATS

LIKES: Nightmares
DISLIKES: Phobia therapy
FRIENDS: Killer Moth
FOES: Batman
SKILLS: Scaring victims
GEAR: Gyro-Copter, Fear gas bombs

FIRST SET: Scarecrow Fearful Face-off
SET NUMBER: 70913
YEAR: 2017

CUT FROM THE WRONG CLOTH

Stitches on fabric face

Rope ties around head sack to make a neck

Suit is the first smart outfit to be worn by a Scarecrow minifigure

THE LAST STRAW

Batman has had enough of Scarecrow's hay-brained plans for releasing toxic fear gas in Gotham City so he chases the villain down in the Tumbler. Which of them will fall apart at the seams?

VITAL STATS

LIKES: Science experiments
DISLIKES: Clearing the air
FRIENDS: None—he'll attack anyone
SKILLS: Chemistry
GEAR: Fear gas

FIRST SET: Batmobile Tumbler: Scarecrow Showdown
SET NUMBER: 76239
YEAR: 2021

DON'T BE FOOLED by Scarecrow's change of appearance. He has smartened up his look with a suit and tie, but one look at his cloth face shows he's still the same sack of straw who thinks it's smart to fool around with fear gas.

POISON IVY
TWISTED BY NATURE

AS TWISTED AS her beloved vines, Poison Ivy just wants to save the environment—from the human race. She can control plants by the power of her mind and is a master of poisons. Don't let her pucker up for a kiss!

A kiss from these sly lips will soon make you snooze

DID YOU KNOW?
A Poison Ivy minifigure from 2012 has lighter green clothes and the same hair piece, but with leaves woven through.

Poison Ivy's leafy costume is also printed on the back

Ivy's body is immune to poison

VITAL STATS
LIKES: Grabbing Batman with the tentacled arms of her mech
DISLIKES: Spinning saw blades
FRIENDS: Firefly
FOES: Batman, The Flash
SKILLS: Controlling plants with her mind
GEAR: Poison-flower shooter, twisted vines, mech

FIRST SET: Batman Mech vs. Poison Ivy Mech
SET NUMBER: 76117
YEAR: 2019

THE ECO-WARRIOR
The 2006 Poison Ivy minifigure has exclusive dark red hair and green lips. Although a brilliant botanist, she would still love to escape her greenhouse-styled prison in Arkham Asylum (set 7785). In 2012, leaves curled through her new red hair.

POISON IN PRISON

Trapped in Arkham Asylum (sct 70912), Poison Ivy is cut off from nature. Her only company is a poster of her beloved plant monster. One flower and some leaves still cling to her dark red hair, but her new outfit leaves a lot to be desired.

White rose clips back new curlier hair

Necklace weaves like tendrils

Poison Ivy's first fabric skirt

VITAL STATS

LIKES: Crashing parties
DISLIKES: Guest lists
FRIENDS: The Joker
FOES: Batman, Commissioner Gordon
SKILLS: Controlling her vine monster
GEAR: 2 twisted vines, vine monster

FIRST SET: The Scuttler
SET NUMBER: 70908
YEAR: 2017

POISON IVY LIKES to be in the middle of the action. She and The Joker don't have invitations to Commissioner Gordon's retirement party, but that doesn't stop them from storming it. Along with her vine monster, Poison Ivy has a blast!

TWO-FACE
SPLIT DOWN THE MIDDLE

VITAL STATS

LIKES: Playing heads or tails
DISLIKES: Matching outfits
FRIENDS: His other half
FOES: Batman
SKILLS: Seeing things from both sides
GEAR: Lucky coin

FIRST SET: The Batmobile: Two-Face's Escape
SET NUMBER: 7781
YEAR: 2006

Two-Face was the first LEGO minifigure to have multicolored hair

Purple facial scarring covers only one side of face

White suit on dark-haired side ... and dark suit on white-haired side

BANDED BANDIT
What's black and white and green all over? A stolen Gotham City Bank truck filled with banknotes and Two-Face's goon. This henchman has a split half black, half white torso but wears plain gray pants.

A LOT OF PEOPLE in Gotham City lead double lives, but Two-Face takes it to extremes! One of the city's biggest crime bosses, he is in two minds about everything and makes decisions by flipping his lucky coin—unlucky for some!

114

TWO-FACE
A MAN DIVIDED

VITAL STATS

LIKES: The number 2
DISLIKES: The acid that caused his facial scarring
FRIENDS: Henchmen
FOES: Batman, bank guards
SKILLS: Bank robbery
GEAR: Lucky two-sided coin, dynamite

FIRST SET: Batmobile and the Two-Face Chase
SET NUMBER: 6864
YEAR: 2012

Scarred face

The original 2006 Two-Face used a LEGO stud as a coin, but this variant is printed

Dynamite is ready to blow

Two-Face's split-color suit continues on the back of his minifigure

LAUGHING ON THE OTHER SIDE OF HIS FACE

By 2017, things have gone from bad to worse for Two-Face. The acid damage on his face has reached down to the bone, and he is locked up in jail. He is on both laundry and sweeping duty—if only he could do two things at once.

TALK ABOUT double trouble. Former District Attorney Harvey Dent still plans his crimes on the flip of his two-headed coin. This updated variant adds crazy color to his originally black-and-white wardrobe.

115

TWO-FACE'S HENCHMAN ONE

HARVEY DENT'S RIGHT-HAND MAN

VITAL STATS

LIKES: Money
DISLIKES: Justice
FRIENDS: Two-Face,
Henchman Two
FOES: Batman
SKILLS: Operating cranes
GEAR: None

FIRST SET: The Batmobile
and The Two-Face Chase
SET NUMBER: 6864
YEAR: 2012

Cool shades—
What every goon
is wearing this
season

A similar color
scheme to his
notorious boss

Torso printed
with zips and
studs

SAFE BREAK!
Henchman One had only one job
on the raid on Gotham Bank—to
make sure that the safe was
safely hoisted clear. What a pity
he forgot to shut the vault door!

FROM AN EARLY AGE, Henchman
One knew he was destined to aid
Gotham City's Super-Villains, and
he soon signed up to work with
Two-Face. You can blame his
mother. What kind of woman calls
her son "Henchman One" anyway?

TWO-FACE'S HENCHMAN TWO
HARVEY DENT'S LEFT-HAND MAN

POOR OLD HENCHMAN

Two has spent his entire life in the shadow of his older twin brother. Henchman Two came a sorry second in every class at goon school, including Tying Up Guards, Blowing Up Safes, and Carrying Swag classes.

The mini knit cap has appeared in more than 90 LEGO sets

Villainous stubble and goatee combo

Henchman Two wears the same jacket as his brother, Henchman One

GETAWAY DRIVER

The one thing Henchman Two can do better than his brother is make a clean getaway— except for that time he left Two-Face's car in a "No Parking" zone and it got towed away.

VITAL STATS

LIKES: A good laugh
DISLIKES: Arkham Asylum
FRIENDS: Two-Face, Henchman One
FOES: Batman
SKILLS: Driving
GEAR: Crowbar

FIRST SET: The Batmobile and The Two-Face Chase
SET NUMBERS: 6864
YEARS: 2012

LIKES: Hedging his bets
DISLIKES: Committing to one color
FRIENDS: Catwoman
FOES: Batman, Robin, Batwoman
SKILLS: Batcave-breaking
GEAR: Dynamite

FIRST SET: Batcave Clayface Invasion
SET NUMBER: 76122
YEAR: 2019

Color line follows the hair's natural wave rather than being centered

Hair is now purple as well as his face

This is the only symmetrical Two-Face torso

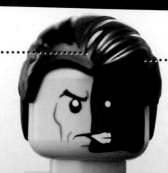

TWO-FACE'S SKIN is getting darker purple and his angry eye redder. He takes his chances without his lucky coin when he joins the raid on the Batcave with Clayface. How will he decide who to finish off first ... Batman or Robin?

SIDE CAR

Like its driver, the Two-Face Excavator has two sides to it; one side has spikes and deadly weapons. It can scoop up that pesky Batman—and even his whole Batcycle. Two-Face has a new minifigure with a half gray and half melted suit.

MR. FREEZE

COLDHEARTED SCIENTIST

VITAL STATS

LIKES: Just chillin'
DISLIKES: Hot tubs
FRIENDS: The Penguin
FOES: Batman and Robin
SKILLS: Freezing things
GEAR: Freeze ray with backpack

FIRST SET: Batcave:
The Penguin and
Mr. Freeze's Invasion
SET NUMBER:
7783
YEAR: 2006

Goggles worn over eyes
that are capable of
producing icy blasts

Helmet keeps this
criminal cool

Freeze ray puts
enemies on ice

STONE-COLD STEAL

Mr. Freeze wields a different freeze
ray as he makes his getaway from a
diamond robbery. Driving a subzero
speedster, he hopes to freeze
Batman's pursuing Buggy in its tracks!

A LAB ACCIDENT permanently
lowered Dr. Victor Fries's body
temperature, forcing him to
wear a special suit of armor at all
times. Now calling himself Mr.
Freeze, he turned to crime to
fund his scientific research.

MR. FREEZE

CHILLED-OUT CRIMINAL

VITAL STATS

LIKES: Turning water to ice
DISLIKES: Winding up in his own ice jail
FRIENDS: Coldhearted folk
FOES: Batman
SKILLS: Riding an ice speeder
GEAR: Ice speeder, freeze ray, ice jail with ice crystal

FIRST SET: Batman vs. Mr. Freeze
SET NUMBER: 10737
YEAR: 2017

Air-conditioning details beneath the armor keep Mr. Freeze chilled

Outfit is a black update of the 2013 blue minifigure

Purple gloves are new

FREEZE RAY

Mr. Freeze's 2013 freeze ray combines a LEGO plate piece with icy blue transparent pieces for freezing action. His bulky armor is suitably high-tech to match.

DR. VICTOR FRIES IS as dangerous as ever, with bulkier armor and an enhanced freeze ray powered by an ice crystal. Since he's been left out in the cold, Mr. Freeze dreams of getting even with those he deems responsible for his frozen condition.

MR. FREEZE

VILLAIN OUT IN THE COLD

New domed helmet with bell jar design

New armored collar

Tubes deliver coolant

VITAL STATS

LIKES: Stomping in his mech
DISLIKES: Frozen joints
FRIENDS: Cool kids
FOES: Batman, Security Guard
SKILLS: Not slipping over
GEAR: Exosuit, stud-shooting freeze ray

FIRST SET: Mr. Freeze Ice Attack
SET NUMBER: 70901
YEAR: 2017

ICY EXOSUIT
Mr. Freeze's new suit and mask are just the tip of the iceberg; he has a whole exosuit to stomp about in. Its huge hands deliver powerful punches and grip his souped-up freeze ray.

MR. FREEZE looks alarmed. Perhaps he has cold feet about his plan to attack Gotham City's Energy Facility? He needs to take a cold, hard look at his wicked ways before he gets into hot water.

MR. FREEZE

STILL AS COLD AS ICE

MR. FREEZE LOOKS less blue these days, but he is still not happy. In fact, he seems distinctly gloomy in his dark new suit. He knows he is on thin ice, being hunted down by Batman in his immense Bat Base on wheels.

Snug, tighter-fitting helmet

Wrinkles on face are like cracking ice

Metallic details on printed tubing

VITAL STATS

LIKES: Freezing his foes
DISLIKES: Electric heaters
FRIENDS: Man-Bat, Bronze Tiger
FOES: Batman, Batgirl, Nightwing
SKILLS: Encasing people in blocks of ice
GEAR: Freeze ray

FIRST SET: Mobile Bat Base
SET NUMBER: 76160
YEAR: 2020

DID YOU KNOW?

These two minifigures wear the updated outfit created for Mr. Freeze by DC Comics in 2016.

COOL DUDE

A similar Mr. Freeze has an elaborate new freeze ray for a magazine giveaway in 2020. The minifigure's neck brace supports the bulky weapon, with tanks of chilled coolant and a tube to deliver it.

Head is encased in a mask so Bane can constantly breathe in Venom

Artificially developed muscles

VITAL STATS

LIKES: Strength-giving Venom
DISLIKES: Prisons
FRIENDS: Poison Ivy
FOES: Batman and Robin
SKILLS: Genius-level intelligence
GEAR: Mole machine

FIRST SET: The Batcave
SET NUMBER: 6860
YEAR: 2012

JUST A LITTLE BIT

The red "B" on Bane's 2016 chest stands for Bane, but it could also be for bad, brawny, and brutal! He might not be at his biggest here, but his Mighty Micros drill tank has a shiny rotating drill bit at the front and flaming chimneys at the back.

No gloves: Bane likes to break things with his bare hands

Black pants replace blue ones from a 2007 variant

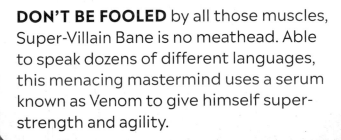

DON'T BE FOOLED by all those muscles, Super-Villain Bane is no meathead. Able to speak dozens of different languages, this menacing mastermind uses a serum known as Venom to give himself super-strength and agility.

BANE

BANE OF BATMAN

Sheepskin collar

Tubes sustain Bane with Venom

Arms and hands of LEGO big-fig are posable

VITAL STATS

LIKES: Venom on tap
DISLIKES: Tube blockages
FRIENDS: Mutant Leader
FOES: Batman
SKILLS: Chemical engineering
GEAR: Toxic truck, toxic bombs, Venom backpack

FIRST SET: Bane Toxic Truck Attack
SET NUMBER: 70914
YEAR: 2017

SUPER-SIZED BANE still wears his trademark mask, even though Venom is now pumped directly into his massive muscly arms. Not one to rely on brute strength, he's armed to the back teeth with toxic waste and has his sights set on Gotham City.

TUMBLER TIME
A more slimline—but still deadly—Bane drives a stolen Tumbler in 2013. His mask is gone, revealing a shaved head and his Venom-breathing apparatus. This minifigure is inspired by Bane in *The Dark Knight Rises* movie.

LEADER OF ASSASSINS

Two-tone hair piece

One face is older and wrinkled; the other side is younger but has crazed yellow eyes

Green version of Martian Manhunter's blue two-piece collared cape

LEADER OF A TEAM of assassins, Rā's al Ghūl's name means "the Demon's Head." You may think his intention of saving the planet is honorable. Unfortunately, his plan for achieving it involves destroying practically everyone.

VITAL STATS

LIKES: Eternal youth
DISLIKES: Batman
FRIENDS: Talia al Ghūl
FOES: Batman, Robin
SKILLS: Assassination
GEAR: Sword

FIRST SET: Batman: Rescue from Rā's al Ghūl
SET NUMBER: 76056
YEAR: 2016

BATH TIME

Regular dips in the translucent-green Lazarus Pit keep Rā's al Ghūl powerful and looking youthful—well, youthful given that he is many centuries old. The downside is, it drives him mad.

VITAL STATS

LIKES: Keeping her options open
DISLIKES: Family ties
FRIENDS: Rā's al Ghūl
FOES: Batman, Robin
SKILLS: Assassination
GEAR: Sword

FIRST SET: Batman: Rescue from Rā's al Ghūl
SET NUMBER: 76056
YEAR: 2016

Black hair piece is also used by Jessica Cruz

Smile is replaced with a fierce scowl on the other side of her head

Unique torso print

SPLIT DECISION
Talia's son, Damian, has become his dad's sidekick, Robin. It's decision time for Talia when he is imprisoned in her dad's desert hideout. It looks like she's not taking her boy wonder's side.

LIFE IS COMPLICATED for Talia. Her loyalty is torn between her evil father, Rā's al Ghūl, and Batman—and their son, Damian Wayne. As her own woman, she is intelligent, a skilled fighter, and an inspiring leader.

ANIMAL MAGNETISM

ENEMIES COME in all shapes and sizes, and some take inspiration from animals or mutants. You might expect these critters in a zoo. Well, they do all belong behind bars!

Mask hides the identity of Catalina Flores

Spider emblem adopted by the vigilante

Muscles honed in her former role as an FBI agent

VITAL STATS

NAME: Tarantula
LIKES: Her own moral code
DISLIKES: Those who disagree with her
FRIENDS: Killer Croc, Zebra-Man
FOES: Batman
SKILLS: Close-quarters combat
GEAR: 2 sai daggers

FIRST SET: Killer Croc Tail-Gator
SET NUMBER: 70907
YEAR: 2017

Mane is the only LEGO mohican piece in black

VITAL STATS

NAME: Zebra-Man
LIKES: Stripes
DISLIKES: Spots
FRIENDS: Killer Croc, Tarantula
FOES: Batman
SKILLS: Horseplay
GEAR: Dynamite

FIRST SET: Killer Croc Tail-Gator
SET NUMBER: 70907
YEAR: 2017

Stripes are caused by magnetic waves

Belt controls Zebra-Man's magnetic powers

127

BEWARE A VILLAIN with a gimmick. Gotham City's enemies have inventive ways of sowing chaos. The Riddler in particular likes to surround himself with these kooky crooks.

Eyes constantly search for glittery things to steal

VITAL STATS

NAME: Magpie
LIKES: Anything shiny, whatever its value
DISLIKES: Anything that isn't shiny
FRIENDS: The Riddler, Kite Man, Calendar Man
FOES: Batman
SKILLS: Feathering her nest with trinkets and diamonds
GEAR: Dynamite

FIRST SET: The Riddler Riddle Racer
SET NUMBER: 70903
YEAR: 2017

Helmet for flying

Armor adopted by Margaret Pye when she became a villain

VITAL STATS

NAME: Kite Man
LIKES: Robberies
DISLIKES: Holes in his kite
FRIENDS: The Riddler, Magpie, Calendar Man
FOES: Batman
SKILLS: Aerodynamic engineering
GEAR: Kite glider

FIRST SET: The Riddler Riddle Racer
SET NUMBER: 70903
YEAR: 2017

Hands clip to kite glider

VITAL STATS

NAME: Calendar Man
LIKES: Holiday-related crimes
DISLIKES: Chaos
FRIENDS: The Riddler, Magpie, Kite Man
FOES: Batman
SKILLS: Mental calculations, scheming
GEAR: Calendar cape

FIRST SET: The Riddler Riddle Racer
SET NUMBER: 70903
YEAR: 2017

Each row represents one week

PETTY CROOKS can be a big threat. Polka-Dot Man and Crazy Quilt may just seem silly, but they can cause serious chaos—and have you ever tried to handcuff a ghost?

VITAL STATS

NAME: Polka-Dot Man
LIKES: Vicious circles
DISLIKES: Corners
FRIENDS: Dotty Super-Villains
FOES: Batman, Robin, Batgirl
SKILLS: Dotty inventions
GEAR: 2 flying discs

FIRST SET: The Ultimate Batmobile
SET NUMBER: 70917
YEAR: 2017

Dots can become getaway saucers

Spandex suit

VITAL STATS

NAME: Gentleman Ghost
LIKES: Holdups
DISLIKES: Not being able to hold anything
FRIENDS: Harley Quinn, Crazy Quilt
FOES: Batgirl
SKILLS: Escaping through walls
GEAR: Cane

FIRST SET: Harley Quinn Cannonball Attack
SET NUMBER: 70921
YEAR: 2018

Outfit of a 19th-century highwayman

The Penguin wears this hat in black

Disorienting print on suit designed to befuddle people

VITAL STATS

NAME: Crazy Quilt
LIKES: Confounding people
DISLIKES: Not seeing the world clearly
FRIENDS: Harley Quinn, Gentleman Ghost
FOES: Batgirl
SKILLS: Hypnosis
GEAR: Dynamite

FIRST SET: Harley Quinn Cannonball Attack
SET NUMBER: 70921
YEAR: 2018

SOME OF Batman's enemies love a good food fight—or an arsenal of food-related superweapons or disguises.

VITAL STATS

NAME: Scarecrow—Pizza Delivery
LIKES: Pizza pranks
DISLIKES: Rude customers
FRIENDS: Pizza chefs
FOES: Batman, Security Guard
SKILLS: Disguise
GEAR: Delivery bike, pizza box, fear gas canister

FIRST SET: Scarecrow Special Delivery
SET NUMBER: 70910
YEAR: 2017

Helmet for riding delivery bike

"Luigi's Pizza" is a front for spreading fear gas

VITAL STATS

NAME: Condiment King
LIKES: Seasoning
DISLIKES: Bland food
FRIENDS: Egghead
FOES: Batman
SKILLS: Causing dangerous slips
GEAR: Condiment shooters

FIRST SET: Egghead Mech Food Fight
SET NUMBER: 70920
YEAR: 2018

Oversized head contains large brain of a criminal mastermind

Fried-egg shaped tie

Straps for backpack that holds canisters

Ketchup

VITAL STATS

NAME: Egghead
LIKES: Eggy puns
DISLIKES: Non-egg themed capers
FRIENDS: Condiment King
FOES: Batman
SKILLS: Creating stinking egg bombs
GEAR: Egghead Mech

FIRST SET: Egghead Mech Food Fight
SET NUMBER: 70920
YEAR: 2018

COLD-BLOODED CROOK

WITH A GRIN to rival The Joker's, this reptilian rascal could snap at any moment! He may not have much in the way of brains, but his tough, scaly skin and super-strength make him the mean, green king of Gotham City's swamps.

Narrowed red eyes

Exclusive scaly face printing

Scales continue on unique torso printing

SCALE MODEL
Killer Croc does his best to outpace the Batboat in this small speedboat. Part of this minifigure's only LEGO set appearance to date, it features exclusive crocodile-face printing and swamp-green missiles.

VITAL STATS

LIKES: Wrestling alligators
DISLIKES: People making fun of his appearance
FRIENDS: The Penguin
FOES: Batman and Robin
SKILLS: Fast healing
GEAR: Speedboat

FIRST SET: The Batboat: Hunt for Killer Croc
SET NUMBER: 7780
YEAR: 2006

KILLER CROC
REPTILIAN ROGUE

VITAL STATS

LIKES: Swamps
DISLIKES: Mirrors
FRIENDS: Tarantula, Zebra-Man
FOES: Batman
SKILLS: Wrestling
GEAR: Tail-Gator truck

FIRST SET: Killer Croc Tail-Gator
SET NUMBER: 70907
YEAR: 2017

Upper jaw is a standard LEGO crocodile piece

LEGO chains attach to studs on manacles

New three-toed feet

CROC AT LARGE
A slightly simpler but equally massive Killer Croc got his teeth into a raid on Gotham City in 2016. He makes a striking entrance on his Battle Chomper, with its deadly swishing tail and giant jaws.

WITH HIS REPTILIAN FEATURES, Killer Croc has always been a genetic rarity, but now he's been super-sized to monstrous proportions as a LEGO big-fig. His new huge, muscular physique is even better for smashing and raiding—some of his favorite hobbies.

COMEBACK CROOK

CAPTAIN BOOMERANG
is an Aussie bloke, but not one you'd want to meet down at the beach. George "Digger" Harkness used to sell toys, but now he trades in misery instead, living a life of crime with his deadly boomerangs.

VITAL STATS

LIKES: Target practice
DISLIKES: The Flash
FRIENDS: Killer Croc, Red Hood, Katana
FOES: Batman
SKILLS: Throwing and catching
GEAR: 2 blue boomerangs

FIRST SET: Batman: Killer Croc Sewer Smash
SET NUMBER: 76055
YEAR: 2016

Trademark long, white scarf

Weaponized boomerangs

Gloves for a good grip

Coat with long tails

SMASHING CITY VISIT
Atop Killer Croc's Battle Chomper, Captain Boomerang is ready to help destroy Gotham City. The vehicle will raze everything in its path, and he will throw his boomerang at anyone who gets in the way.

MERCENARY THIEF

VITAL STATS

LIKES: Diamonds
DISLIKES: Being chased
FRIENDS: Harley Quinn
FOES: Batman, Robin
SKILLS: Piloting his jetboat
GEAR: Jetpack, bazooka

FIRST SET: Batboat Harbor Pursuit
SET NUMBER: 76034
YEAR: 2015

Two-color orange and black mask

Spare ammo ready for any mission

Two-tone legs

MASKED MAN

The reverse of Deathstroke's mask features his trademark long headband that the mercenary sometimes wears in the comic books. His bandolier can be seen wrapping around the back of the minifigure.

BEFORE TURNING TO CRIME, Slade Wilson was a marine who was transformed into a soldier by the US military. Tackling weapon-expert Deathstroke is always dangerous, especially when he's on the run from his latest diamond heist.

DEADSHOT
MASKED MARKSMAN

Targeting sight built into mask

Armored suit can withstand explosions

DID YOU KNOW?
Deadshot made his comic book debut in *Batman #59* in 1950.

JETTING OFF
Deadshot is really skyrocketing with this jetpack and bazooka combo! The giant weapon is made from eight pieces and can fire studs on Batman and his friends below.

Wrist-mounted weapons

VITAL STATS

LIKES: Moving targets
DISLIKES: Feeling aimless
FRIENDS: Harley Quinn
FOES: Batman
SKILLS: Expert aim
GEAR: Built-in weapons and targeting tech

FIRST SET: Batman: Gotham City Cycle Chase
SET NUMBER: 76053
YEAR: 2016

THIS SHARPSHOOTER likes to boast that he never misses a target. He wears a metal mask with a special eyepiece to help him take aim and has weapons built in to the arms of his suit. Sometimes he fights crime, but he prefers to battle Batman!

FIREFLY

AERIAL ARSONIST

GARFIELD LYNNS just loved setting things on fire. He made a career of it, creating blazing stunts for Hollywood films. But when that wasn't enough to quench his thirst for fire, he made his own flamethrower and took to the skies as the villain Firefly.

Printed red eyes

Regular minifigure facial expression under the mask

Jetpack enables flight like a firefly

Costume is bright like a firefly's glowing abdomen

VITAL STATS

LIKES: Fire
DISLIKES: Water
FRIENDS: Poison Ivy
FOES: Batman, The Flash
SKILLS: Setting anything ablaze
GEAR: Jetpack, flamethrower

FIRST SET: Batman Mech vs. Poison Ivy Mech
SET NUMBER: 76117
YEAR: 2019

FIRING ON ALL CYLINDERS

Firefly is all fired up and ready to go after the Fastest Man Alive. But with the net from Batman's mech headed his way, it looks like he might crash and burn.

TALON
ELITE ASSASSIN

Collection of knives in bandolier

BEWARE THE TALONS. These highly trained assassins and experts in stealth move invisibly around Gotham City. Enhanced with electrum by their masters, the Court of Owls, they have superhuman powers, including the ability to heal.

Symbol of the Court of Owls

Claws are highly effective in combat

Black outfit for melting into shadows

VITAL STATS

LIKES: Catching people by surprise
DISLIKES: Cold temperatures
FRIENDS: Other Talons
FOES: Batman
SKILLS: Hand-to-hand combat, stealth
GEAR: Ninja swords, holster backpack, claws

FIRST SET: Batman: The Attack of the Talons
SET NUMBER: 76110
YEAR: 2018

DOUBLE TROUBLE
It takes two Talons to take on Batman in his bike—one with knives and the other with two katana swords. Perhaps Ace the Bat-Hound's dogged determination will hound them out of town?

AN OMAC (Observational Metahuman Activity Construct) is a soldier in powerful and almost indestructible cybernetic armor. Armies of OMACs are programmed by the all-seeing Brother Eye supercomputer to carry out its evil bidding.

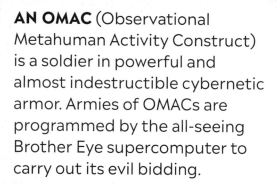

Eye fires energy beams

Programming in head interfaces with hive mind

Mark of the Brother Eye supercomputer

VITAL STATS

LIKES: Instructions
DISLIKES: Free will
FRIENDS: All the other OMACs
FOES: Batman, Batwoman
SKILLS: Flight, super-strength and speed
GEAR: 2 red power blasts

FIRST SET: Batman: Brother Eye Takedown
SET NUMBER: 76111
YEAR: 2018

FOLLOWING ORDERS
When Brother Eye instructs OMAC to attack Batwoman, OMAC does just that. His power blasts fire straight at her Batjet. With his robust robotic powers, he doesn't fear her shooters.

KILLER MOTH

FLY IN THE OINTMENT

Mask with antennae

Red eye cover under mask

Fairy wings turned transparent orange for this minifigure

Moth emblem

Suit enables him to fly

VITAL STATS

LIKES: Attention
DISLIKES: Not being taken seriously
FRIENDS: Scarecrow
FOES: Batman, Blue Beetle
SKILLS: Small-time crime
GEAR: Wings, cocoon weapon

FIRST SET: Batman: Scarecrow Harvest of Fear
SET NUMBER: 76054
YEAR: 2016

MOTH RACER

Killer Moth loves his gadgets. His short-legged Mighty Micros minifigure rests his wings by driving his bug car, complete with minifigure-head bug eyes and a goblet-piece proboscis.

PETTY CROOK DRURY WALKER took to crime like a moth to a flame, but he wanted more. Determined to be a worthy adversary of Batman, he became Killer Moth, equipped with moth wings, a mask, and a cocoon weapon.

139

MAN-BAT

GOTHAM CITY'S NIGHTMARE

VITAL STATS

LIKES: Biology
DISLIKES: People who mumble
FRIENDS: Bronze Tiger, Mr. Freeze
FOES: Batman, Batgirl, Nightwing
SKILLS: Sonar abilites
GEAR: Dynamite

FIRST SET: Mobile Bat Base
SET NUMBER: 76160
YEAR: 2020

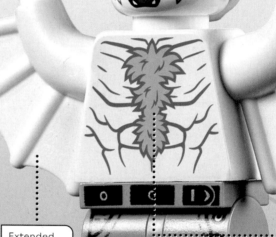

Man-Bat's head piece hides an alternate worried face

Extended batwings move with arms

New fur is white and gray unlike the first version, which was brown

GOING BATTY

Whenever Dr. Langstrom transforms into Man-Bat, he becomes a wild beast capable of dropping dynamite on the unsuspecting heads of Gotham City's citizens.

WHEN BRUCE WAYNE'S biologist friend Dr. Kirk Langstrom realized that he was going deaf, he created a serum that would give him the extraordinary hearing of bats. It worked, but also transformed him into a hideous batlike monster!

BEHIND THE MASK of Bronze Tiger is a man named Ben Turner and a lot of rage. Ben tried to control his fury by channeling it into martial arts, but it boiled over. Bronze Tiger became a criminal, and Batman is the focus of his wrath now.

Hood of sweater printed on the back

Teeth worn around neck

Roaring tiger belt buckle

Claw pieces shared with Katana's minifigure

VITAL STATS

LIKES: Challenging people to a fight
DISLIKES: Anyone who gets in his way
FRIENDS: Man-Bat, Mr. Freeze
FOES: Batman, Batgirl, Nightwing
SKILLS: Martial arts
GEAR: Claws

FIRST SET: Mobile Bat Base
SET NUMBER: 76160
YEAR: 2020

EASY TIGER
When do-gooder Super Heroes come hunting you down in their huge Mobile Bat Base, what else can you do but fight back? Nightwing tries to capture Bronze Tiger, so the cat gets his claws out.

CHAPTER FIVE

JUSTICE LEAGUE AND THEIR ALLIES

WONDER WOMAN

STARFIRE

HAWKMAN

GREEN LANTERN

GUYS, THE GRASS LOOKS GREENER OVER THERE.

THE FLASH

JUSTICE LEAGUE FOUNDER

Wings built into more aerodynamic helmet

Flesh-colored face printed onto red element

VITAL STATS

LIKES: The Speed Force
DISLIKES: Forces beyond his control
FRIENDS: Batman
FOES: Parademons
SKILLS: Electrical manipulation
GEAR: Power blasts

FIRST SET: Knightcrawler Tunnel Attack
SET NUMBER: 76086
YEAR: 2017

DID YOU KNOW?

This version of Barry Allen's costume is from the 2017 movie *Justice League*.

REVERSE-FLASH

Although equally as fast as The Flash, the yellow-suited Reverse-Flash is his opposite in intent and color. He is the corrupted genius Professor Eobard Thawne who uses the Speed Force to track down and battle The Flash.

Red suit is darker than previous variants

BLINK AND YOU COULD miss Barry Allen as The Flash in his new aerodynamic suit, rippling with Speed Force energy. As a founding member of the Justice League, the Central City speedster is always quick to leap to humanity's defense against Super-Villainous threats.

VITAL STATS

LIKES: Speed
DISLIKES: Staying still
FRIENDS: Batman
FOES: Poison Ivy, Firefly
SKILLS: Superhuman speed
GEAR: Orange power burst

FIRST SET: Batman Mech vs. Poison Ivy Mech
SET NUMBER: 76117
YEAR: 2019

Wings on mask are a symbol of his speed

Lightning bolt hints at how Barry Allen became The Flash

Dual-molded legs are unique to this Flash—his two previous variants have plain red legs

THE NEED FOR SPEED
The Scarlet Speedster's first minifigure was on hand to help Batman chase down The Riddler's dragster in 2014. With his acrobatic abilities, he jumps over The Riddler's bombs (and bananas) and remains in hot pursuit of the questionable criminal.

AFTER HE WAS STRUCK by lightning, police scientist Barry Allen developed the power to run at high speeds. Able to outrun anything on the planet, The Flash rushed into a life battling for justice as the resident crime fighter of Central City.

DID YOU KNOW?
The Flash appears in the LEGO® Batman™ 2: DC Comics Super Heroes and LEGO® Batman™ 3: Beyond Gotham video games.

145

VITAL STATS

LIKES: Acceleration
DISLIKES: Dawdlers
FRIENDS: Slowcoaches
FOES: Mr. Freeze
SKILLS: Quick thinking
GEAR: Lightning speed bolts

FIRST SET: Collectible LEGO® DC Super Heroes Minifigures Series
SET NUMBER: 71026
YEAR: 2020

World War I helmet with wings like the Roman god Mercury

Lightning-shaped speed bolts

Blue pants are unique to Jay Garrick's Flash

JAY GARRICK WAS the original speedster. After a lab accident exposed him to the Speed Force in the 1940s, Jay donned his father's helmet and became The Flash to fight crime. He even teamed up with Barry Allen's Flash when he traveled to the future.

DID YOU KNOW?

Jason "Jay" Garrick first appeared in a comic as The Flash in 1940.

FLASH DRIVE

This 2016 Mighty Micros race car might not be as fast as The Flash himself, but it gives Barry Allen's little legs a rest while he enjoys his can of Power Bolt energy drink!

AQUAMAN
CROWN PRINCE OF ATLANTIS

FROZEN FISH
The first Aquaman minifigure, from 2013, has longer hair and a somber as well as an angry expression. He has plenty of time to think when he is put on ice in Mr. Freeze's petrifying polar prison.

Blonde version of Bruce Wayne's swept-back hair piece

Eyes can adjust to see in the dark

Aquaman's muscles are also printed on the back of the minifigure

VITAL STATS

LIKES: The ocean
DISLIKES: Ice prisons
FRIENDS: Arctic Batman, Robin
FOES: Mr. Freeze, Black Manta
SKILLS: Breathing underwater
GEAR: Trident

FIRST SET: Aquaman and Storm
SET NUMBER: 75996
YEAR: 2018

HALF HUMAN AND HALF ATLANTEAN, Aquaman tirelessly defends Earth's oceans from attack. The briny ruler is able to communicate telepathically with fish and sea mammals and was one of the founding members of the Justice League.

147

AQUAMAN

JUSTICE FIGHTER

DID YOU KNOW?

Aquaman's appearance in the *Justice League* (2017) and *Aquaman* (2018) movies is the inspiration for his two dark-haired minifigures.

IN DEEP WATER

Parademons come searching Atlantis for a Mother Box that will give them huge power. Aquaman battles them alongside two Atlantean Guards, who wear golden, spiny fish helmets.

Previously blond hair is now dark with highlights

Ancient Atlantean armor was first worn by King Atlan

VITAL STATS

LIKES: Peace
DISLIKES: Invaders
FRIENDS: Mera
FOES: Black Manta
SKILLS: Protecting the oceans
GEAR: Trident, power blasts

FIRST SET: Black Manta Strike
SET NUMBER: 76095
YEAR: 2018

A SON OF THE LAND and a king of the sea, Aquaman bridges two realms in one world. The marine muscleman protects the oceans from many threats—humans, extraterrestrial invaders, and his archnemesis, Black Manta.

AQUAMAN
UNDERWATER RULER

VITAL STATS

LIKES: Hand accessories
DISLIKES: Piranhas
FRIENDS: Fish
FOES: Fishermen
SKILLS: Communicating with fish
GEAR: Fish, hook hand

FIRST SET: Collectible LEGO® DC Super Heroes Minifigures Series
SET NUMBER: 71026
YEAR: 2020

AFTER LOSING his hand in an unfortunate piranha incident, Aquaman now has a harpoon replacement. Along with long, blond, seaweedy hair and scaly armor, this minifigure is definitely no landlubber!

Fish-scale armor

CLASH OF THE TRIDENTS

Power Bursts shoot Aquaman's 2019 minifigure through the water. But unfortunately for him, his half brother, the Ocean Master, has them, too. The battle for the throne of Atlantis is a family affair.

DID YOU KNOW?

Aquaman was born Arthur Curry and he was raised by his human dad in a lighthouse.

MERA
SEA ROYALTY

Eyes see well in dark depths

DID YOU KNOW?
Mera's minifigure shares a hair mold with Lois Lane and The Cheetah and a face print with Vicki Vale.

QUEEN OF AN underwater world in another dimension, Mera teams up with Aquaman to defeat common threats to their life under the ocean waves. She can direct water and shape it into solid objects, just with the power of her thoughts.

Water channeled into Power Blasts

Shiny, fish-scale-inspired design

VITAL STATS

LIKES: Calm seas
DISLIKES: Invasions
FRIENDS: Aquaman
FOES: Black Manta
SKILLS: Hydrokinetics
GEAR: Power Blasts

FIRST SET: Black Manta Strike
SET NUMBER: 76095
YEAR: 2018

WATER FIGHT
Any quarrel with Aquaman is a quarrel with Mera. So when Black Manta strikes at Atlantis, Mera battles him, using her mind to launch concussive water blasts at his sinister Sub.

Golden helmet also winged to be aerodynamic

BEATING WINGS

Hawkman comes with two sets of plastic wings, one spread out for flight and the other drawn in for fight! There's also a two-sided head beneath that golden helmet.

Wings attach to Hawkman's minifigure using gold studs

Hawk symbol joins crossing chest straps

VITAL STATS

LIKES: Flying high
DISLIKES: Having his wings clipped
FRIENDS: Superman, Cyborg, Green Arrow
FOES: Darkseid
SKILLS: Flight
GEAR: Wings, mace

FIRST SET: Darkseid Invasion
SET NUMBER: 76028
YEAR: 2015

ARCHAEOLOGIST CARTER HALL uses magical Nth Metal to soar through the air as the savage Hawkman. This Justice League member is no young featherweight—he's actually a reincarnated Egyptian prince!

HAWKGIRL

FEATHERED FIGHTER

VITAL STATS

LIKES: Fighting for a worthy cause
DISLIKES: A quiet life
FRIENDS: Superman, El Dorado, Green Arrow
FOES: Hawkers
SKILLS: Flight
GEAR: Mace, wings

FIRST SET: The Justice League Anniversary Party
SET NUMBER: 70919
YEAR: 2018

Battle helmet identical to Hawkman's

Belt made of Nth metal

Wings are not part of a suit but grow naturally

HAWK BY NAME and hawk by nature! Thanagarians live for war so Hawkgirl never questioned what lay in store for her future. She followed in the ferocious footsteps of her family, and she found worthy teammates in the Justice League.

PARTY ANIMALS

Happy Birthday to the Justice League! Hawkgirl swaps her mace for her dancing shoes as the group celebrates their anniversary. Ace the Bat-Hound plays the music as the DJ—the Dog Jiver.

DID YOU KNOW?

Hawkgirl has been the Super Hero persona of three people: Shiera Saunders, Kendra Saunders, and Shayera Hol.

GUARDIAN OF EARTH

VITAL STATS

LIKES: Protecting the Earth
DISLIKES: Losing his Lantern
FRIENDS: Batman
FOES: Sinestro
SKILLS: Space flight
GEAR: Green Lantern

FIRST SET: Green Lantern vs. Sinestro
SET NUMBER: 76025
YEAR: 2015

Green Lantern shares a hair piece with Commissioner Gordon

Two-sided head features a grinning face on the reverse

Green Lantern uniform complete with the insignia of the Lantern Corps

Black printing continues on the back

DOWN-TO-EARTH
An earlier Green Lantern, based on the 2011 *Green Lantern* movie, was given away to 1,500 raffle winners at the 2011 San Diego Comic-Con, with a smaller quantity released at New York Comic-Con the same year.

WHEN TEST PILOT Hal Jordan discovered the wreckage of an alien spacecraft he received a power ring that transformed him into the Green Lantern. Drawing power from his cosmic lantern, Hal protects the solar system from attack.

GREEN LANTERN

EXTRATERRESTRIAL POLICE

Green eyes unique to this Lantern minifigure

DID YOU KNOW?
John Stewart's minifigure and his emerald spacecraft were created exclusively for the LEGO® DC Comics *Super Heroes Build Your Own Adventure* book.

EVERY SECTOR needs a Green Lantern to protect it—and a backup. John Stewart was just a regular person when the Guardians chose him as Hal Jordan's deputy. When Hal is injured, John steps up as Earth's primary Green Lantern.

Green Lantern symbol on a new suit

VITAL STATS

LIKES: Building constructs
DISLIKES: Earth invaders
FRIENDS: Batman, Superman, The Flash
FOES: Enemies of the Justice League
SKILLS: Master builder
GEAR: Spaceship, hammer construct

FIRST SET: LEGO *DC Comics Super Heroes Build Your Own Adventure*
SET NUMBER: N/A
YEAR: 2017

IMAGINE THAT!
As Green Lantern, John Stewart can use energy channeled through his power ring to make solid constructs of anything he imagines— like this spaceship. But it works only when he's concentrating!

Full head mask

DID YOU KNOW?
Guy Gardner, another Green Lantern, appears as a minifigure in the LEGO *Batman* 3 video game.

New short-sleeved Green Lantern suit

JESSICA CRUZ
Hal Jordan combines Jessica Cruz's power battery with Simon Baz's, so the two Green Lanterns have to work together as partners—whether they like it or not.

VITAL STATS

LIKES: Street racings
DISLIKES: Bullies
FRIENDS: Green Lantern Jessica Cruz
FOES: Yellow Lantern Corps
SKILLS: Emerald sight—seeing glimpses of the future
GEAR: Lantern, ring

FIRST SET: Collectible LEGO DC Super Heroes Minifigures Series
SET NUMBER: 71026
YEAR: 2020

A ROCKY START in life saw Simon Baz flirt with the wrong side of the law, but he then became the Green Lantern of Sector 2814, swearing the Green Lantern oath to defend Earth. Now he attracts a different type of trouble!

GREEN ARROW

ANGRY ARCHER

VITAL STATS

LIKES: Shooting straight
DISLIKES: A close shave
FRIENDS: Superman, Cyborg
FOES: Darkseid
SKILLS: Archery
GEAR: Longbow

FIRST SET: Darkseid Invasion
SET NUMBER: 76028
YEAR: 2015

Face stubble printing reveals that the Green Archer is in need of a shave

Green plastic hood hangs from around the neck

Standard LEGO® bow and arrow in green

ARMED AND DANGEROUS

You can swivel the Green Arrow's head to reveal an angry expression. A quiver full of arrows is also printed on the back of his torso, beneath his cape.

WITH A BODY SIMILAR to the earlier San Diego Comic-Con exclusive, this Green Arrow has plain green legs rather than kneepads. Luckily for the Justice League, the Arrow stays on target no matter what his workday wardrobe.

GREEN ARROW

THE EMERALD ARCHER

Playful feather in his LEGO Forestman's cap

Blond goatee

Dark green quiver attaches around the neck

"G" belt buckle

VITAL STATS

LIKES: Hitting the bull's-eye
DISLIKES: Inviting Batman to the party
FRIENDS: Superman, Hawkgirl, El Dorado, Wonder Dog
FOES: Party poopers
SKILLS: Archery
GEAR: Bow and arrow, quiver

FIRST SET: The Justice League Anniversary Party
SET NUMBER: 70919
YEAR: 2018

QUICK OFF THE MARK
In 2013, 200 exclusive Green Arrow minifigures with a dark-green hood were raffled at Comic-Con. They are based on Green Arrow's updated 2011 costume from the comics.

IT'S PARTY TIME, and the Green Arrow's new target is the dance floor. With high boots, lime-green tights, and a lace-up tunic, he has the look of a classic archer—and the moves of a dance-floor fiend.

SHAPESHIFTING ALIEN

Single-sided green head

Exclusive blue collar for this shapeshifter from Mars

VITAL STATS

LIKES: Cookies
DISLIKES: Eating meat
FRIENDS: Superman, Supergirl
FOES: Brainiac
SKILLS: Able to change his shape
GEAR: None

FIRST SET: Brainiac Attack
SET NUMBER: 76040
YEAR: 2015

Body printing on front and back based on the Martian Manhunter's classic costume

ALTERNATE ALIEN
An earlier version of the Martian Manhunter minifigure was given away on LEGO.com in March 2014. This one had a costume based on the 2011 comic books, plus a simplified blue cape.

THE LAST SURVIVOR OF a Martian race, J'onn J'onzz came to Earth to join the Justice League. Able to recover from just about any injury, the Martian Manhunter can take on any form he chooses to solve crimes. He is also a mind reader!

PLASTIC MAN

THE STRETCHABLE SUPER HERO

Plastic Man shares a hair piece with Superman

Those goggles make Plastic Man one cool dude—or so he thinks

VITAL STATS

LIKES: Pranks, the Justice League
DISLIKES: Being overstretched
FRIENDS: Batman
FOES: Enemies of the Justice League
SKILLS: Stretching into any shape he wishes
GEAR: None

FIRST SET: Plastic Man
SET NUMBER: 5004081
YEAR: 2014

GIVEN AWAY at GameStop stores with preorders of LEGO® Batman™ 3: Beyond Gotham, this exclusive minifigure gave super-stretchy Patrick "Eel" O'Brian a fantastic plastic form. Plastic Man has the power to reshape his body.

Boots printed on red legs

DID YOU KNOW?

Eel O'Brian was a criminal who fell in a vat of chemicals during a heist. It gave him a stretchy body—and a conscience.

A QUICK CHANGE

Plastic Man's costume is also printed on the back. The outfit was inspired by Plastic Man's updated appearance in the 2011 Flashpoint event. This was Plastic Man's first appearance with tights instead of bare legs.

TURN LEAD into gold? No problem for Firestorm! Tinkering with materials on an atomic level has been second nature to this hero ever since he was created in a lab accident. It fused together a high-school athlete and brainbox science student.

Transparent flames attached to unique head piece

Blazing flames shoot from head

VITAL STATS

LIKES: Atomic chemistry
DISLIKES: Enemies of the Justice League
FRIENDS: Batman, Wonder Woman
FOES: Lex Luthor, The Cheetah
SKILLS: Flight, altering inorganic materials
GEAR: Orange Power Bursts

FIRST SET: Lex Luthor Mech Takedown
SET NUMBER: 76097
YEAR: 2018

Design on torso echoes atomic structures

Red for scorching power

CHAIN REACTION
As a member of the Justice League, Firestorm battles Lex Luthor's mech alongside Batman and Wonder Woman. He flies into action, shooting sizzling orange flames from his feet and Power Bursts from his hands.

ATOM

TEENY-WEENY SUPER HERO

DID YOU KNOW?

This variant of Atom is based on his appearance in the *Arrowverse* TV shows *Arrow* and *DC's Legends of Tomorrow*.

Double-sided face looks happy and fierce

Exosuit is engineered to keep Atom alive when he shrinks

Gloves contain emergency backup mechanisms

VITAL STATS

LIKES: Miniature things
DISLIKES: Living it large
FRIENDS: Hawkman
FOES: Darkseid
SKILLS: Shrinking
GEAR: None

FIRST SET: Atom
SET NUMBER: SDCC2016
YEAR: 2016

SIZE MATTERS

Brilliant scientist Ray Palmer goes small but thinks big, and Palmer Technologies is his cutting-edge company. Atom's set was a San Diego Comic-Con exclusive, given away in a raffle.

MINIFIGURES ARE MINI-SIZED, but they're huge to Ray Palmer when he becomes Atom. The Super Hero shrinks to such infinitesimal proportions that he can travel down phone lines and around people's bloodstreams.

ARSENAL
THE RED ARROW

VITAL STATS

LIKES: Fighting crime
DISLIKES: Being called Speedy
FRIENDS: Green Arrow
FOES: Deathstroke
SKILLS: Archery
GEAR: Longbow

FIRST SET: Arsenal
SET NUMBER: SDCC2015
YEAR: 2015

Red hood based on the costume from the *Arrow* TV show

Leather straps printed on chest

Black version of Green Arrow's longbow

READY TO FIRE
The back of the exclusive minifigure shows a quiver of arrows ready to fire. Arsenal also has a double-sided head complete with a snarling face on the reverse.

WHEN ARROW TOOK martial arts expert Roy Harper under his wing, he tried to call his new sidekick Speedy. Harper hated the name, calling himself Arsenal instead. The young archer is almost as good a shot as his green-hooded mentor.

ELECTRIC POWERHOUSE

JEFFERSON PIERCE IS the epitome of people power. Crackling with electricity, he uses his energy to fight crime as Black Lightning. He is amped up to protect the ordinary people in his neighborhood who are suffering at the hands of a criminal gang.

Lightning motif

Ripples of electrical energy

DID YOU KNOW?

In 1977, Black Lightning became the first African American Super Hero to have his own DC comic book series.

Suit helps Jefferson control his powers

Stylish outfit for power dressing

VITAL STATS

LIKES: Shock attacks
DISLIKES: Power outages
FRIENDS: Justice League
FOES: Criminals
SKILLS: Creating and controlling electricity
GEAR: None

FIRST SET: Black Lightning
SET NUMBER: SDCC2018
YEAR: 2018

BOLT FROM THE BLUE

Black Lightning charged the atmosphere at San Diego Comic-Con in 2018 when he was given away as an exclusive promotional minifigure.

163

MISTER MIRACLE

SYMBOL OF FREEDOM

VITAL STATS

LIKES: Alien technology
DISLIKES: Imprisonment
FRIENDS: Superman
FOES: Darkseid
SKILLS: Escapology
GEAR: Chains, handcuffs

FIRST SET: Collectible LEGO DC Super Heroes Minifigures Series
SET NUMBER: 71026
YEAR: 2020

Mask has circuitry for the Mother Box and life-support systems

Boots contain laser jets

POWER SOURCE

Mister Miracle has his Mother Box to thank for his miraculous abilities. He harnesses power from this part-living computer, which draws energy from the mysterious Source.

DO YOU BELIEVE in miracles? The alien Scott Free did, and he escaped his terrible life and got a new start on Earth. Mister Miracle has the astounding skills of a circus escape artist, wowing crowds by shedding his ever more elaborate shackles.

Blonde hair piece shared with the 2015 variant of Supergirl

Double-sided face print has a smile with and without teeth

Patriotic stars link to the US "Stars and Stripes" flag

Printed Utility Belt

VITAL STATS

LIKES: Making a difference
DISLIKES: Publicity stunts
FRIENDS: Superman
FOES: Lex Luthor
SKILLS: Martial arts and gymnastics
GEAR: Cosmic Staff

FIRST SET: Collectible LEGO DC Super Heroes Minifigures Series
SET NUMBER: 71026
YEAR: 2020

RISING STAR
Cutting her teeth as the Star-Spangled Kid, Courtney Whitmore then graduated to Star Girl. Her stepfather was the crime fighter Stripesy, but she makes her own name without riding on his cape-tails.

STAR GIRL CARRIES THE Cosmic Staff, which passed to her from Starman (Jack Knight) after his retirement. Suffused with stellar energy, the weapon bestows her with powers like flight, energy manipulation, blasts, and levitation.

HUNTRESS
DEADLY DAUGHTER

VITAL STATS

LIKES: Her dad's heroic acts
DISLIKES: Her mom's criminality
FRIENDS: Her dad, mostly
FOES: Her mom, mostly
SKILLS: Sharpshooting
GEAR: Crossbow

FIRST SET: Collectible LEGO DC Super Heroes Minifigures Series
SET NUMBER: 71026
YEAR: 2020

Purple mask is a link to her mother's costume

DID YOU KNOW?
This variant of Huntress's costume is based on her comic book look that began in 2012.

Purple Utility Belt piece shared with Catwoman and Roller Disco Batman

Cape with a single hole rather than the more common two-holed Super Hero cape

IN HER SIGHTS
Crime-fighting Huntress has many strings to her bow, including hand-to-hand combat and gymnastics. Her trademark weapon is her crossbow, and she carries a metallic dark-gray version.

WHEN YOUR DAD is Bruce Wayne and your mom is Selina Kyle, there's a good chance you'll don a cape, too—but as a Super Hero or a Super-Villain? Helena Wayne follows her dad as a vigilante named Huntress. Criminals are her quarry.

METAMORPHO
ELEMENT MAN

DID YOU KNOW?
Metamorpho belongs to a race of metamorphae created by the Ancient Egyptian sun god, Ra.

SINCE BEING EXPOSED to a radioactive meteorite, Rex Mason can alter his physique into any element contained in the human body. He can shapeshift and be solid, liquid, plasma, or gas—or several states at once.

Hands often take the form of useful tools and weapons

"M" belt buckle

Blue underpants

Ice leg

Leg made of mud

VITAL STATS

LIKES: Makeovers
DISLIKES: Inflexible thinking
FRIENDS: The elements
FOES: Villains
SKILLS: Shapeshifting
GEAR: Giant fist

FIRST SET: Collectible LEGO DC Super Heroes Minifigures Series
SET NUMBER: 71026
YEAR: 2020

TOOLS OF THE TRADE
Never mind the right gadget for the job, Metamorpho has the right body part. He can shapeshift his hands into any gizmo. Can opener? No problem! Giant fist? How does magenta suit you?

THE WORLD'S MIGHTIEST MORTAL

AT AGE TEN, Billy Batson was granted magical powers by a wizard. By shouting "Shazam!" Billy changes into a powerful being blessed with the ability of legendary heroes Solomon, Hercules, Atlas, Zeus, Achilles, and Mercury (spelling "Shazam").

DID YOU KNOW?

Shazam appears in the video games LEGO *Batman 2: DC Comics Super Heroes*, LEGO *Batman 3: Beyond Gotham*, and LEGO *DC Super-Villains*.

Shazam shares a hair piece with Bruce Wayne

Printed body emblazoned with lightning strike

VITAL STATS

LIKES: Being a hero
DISLIKES: Being a kid
FRIENDS: The Justice League
FOES: Black Adam
SKILLS: Magical abilities
GEAR: White cape

FIRST SET: SHAZAM!
SET NUMBER: 30623
YEAR: 2019

Shazam wears one of the longest capes to appear on a LEGO DC minifigure

SEEING RED

The first Shazam minifigure was a Comic-Con exclusive in 2012, and he shared a hair piece with the 2012 Bruce Wayne. Although he is shouting angrily here, the other side of Shazam's head is calm.

SHAZAM!

LITTLE KID-TURNED-CHAMPION-OF-MAGIC

Black hair has been swapped for a white hood

Spongy-style cape

Metallic gold belt

DID YOU KNOW?

In 2020, a shinier-caped version of this Shazam was a magazine exclusive.

VITAL STATS

LIKES: Helping Batman
DISLIKES: Zapping baddies
FRIENDS: Batman, Commissioner Gordon
FOES: The Riddler
SKILLS: Flying, lightning blasts
GEAR: 2 Power Bursts

FIRST SET: Batwing and The Riddler Heist
SET NUMBER: 76120
YEAR: 2019

JUST SAY THE WORD

In 2019, Billy Batson cries, "Shazam!" to trigger his powers. He gives Commissioner Gordon and Batman a boost in foiling The Riddler's pilfering plans in Batwing and The Riddler Heist (76120).

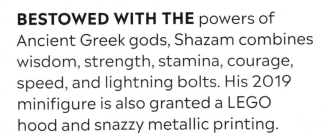

BESTOWED WITH THE powers of Ancient Greek gods, Shazam combines wisdom, strength, stamina, courage, speed, and lightning bolts. His 2019 minifigure is also granted a LEGO hood and snazzy metallic printing.

169

VITAL STATS

LIKES: Honesty
DISLIKES: Lies
FRIENDS: Etta Candy
FOES: The Cheetah
SKILLS: Advanced fighting techniques
GEAR: Lasso of Truth

FIRST SET: Superman vs. Power Armor Lex
SET NUMBER: 6862
YEAR: 2012

Hair piece includes Wonder Woman's golden tiara

A turn of her head shows how angry she is to be captured by Lex Luthor

NOTHING TO SEE HERE!
Wonder Woman built the Invisible Jet in the name of peace. By traveling unseen, she can carry out her missions without starting a fight. Her translucent Mighty Micro jet spars with Doomsday.

Wonder Woman's costume is based on the flag of the United States of America

BORN ON PARADISE ISLAND,
Amazonian Princess Diana trained to be a warrior from the moment she could fight. The strongest woman on the planet, she now fights crime as a member of the Justice League.

WONDER WOMAN

GOLDEN AGE HERO

HARKING BACK TO the Golden Age of comics, Wonder Woman sports her classic costume from her very first appearance in *Sensation Comics* #1 in 1942. The Amazonian warrior arrives in America and takes the identity of a nurse named Diana Prince.

Golden eagle is a symbol of the United States of America

Indestructible bracelets

Removable skirt piece with star-printed shorts underneath

Lasso of Truth

VITAL STATS

LIKES: Vintage costumes
DISLIKES: Modern fashions
FRIENDS: Justice League
FOES: Gorilla Grodd, Mr. Freeze
SKILLS: Navigating the world of people
GEAR: Lasso of Truth

FIRST SET: Collectible LEGO® DC Super Heroes Minifigures Series
SET NUMBER: 71026
YEAR: 2020

VEXED BY LEX

Teaming up with the Justice League, can the Amazonian's 2018 minifigure get the Energy Infuser back from Lex Luthor? She wears a printed skirt and has a stylized eagle that's beginning to look like a "W."

WONDER WOMAN

WARRIOR FROM THEMYSCIRA

This Wonder Woman minifigure is the only one to have long sleeves

THE DAUGHTER OF

Hippolyta, Queen of the Amazons, and Zeus, the leader of the Gods of Olympus, Wonder Woman is imbued with immense powers. She also wields a magical lasso that compels people to tell the whole truth.

"W" belt has a mix of reflective and matt gold printing

VITAL STATS

LIKES: The truth
DISLIKES: Liars
FRIENDS: None
FOES: None
SKILLS: Getting the truth out of people
GEAR: Lasso of Truth

FIRST SET: LEGO *DC Comics Super Heroes: The Awesome Guide*
SET NUMBER: N/A
YEAR: 2017

DID YOU KNOW?

This exclusive minifigure is based on an updated comic book costume that first featured in 2015.

SILVER BULLET

Fighting crime in a modern age, the 2015 Wonder Woman minifigure, with silver printing, is based on a costume introduced to the comics in 2011. Villains beware, this Wonder Woman is ready for battle.

VITAL STATS

LIKES: Animals
DISLIKES: War
FRIENDS: Steve Trevor
FOES: Ares
SKILLS: Hand-to-hand combat
GEAR: Amazonian sword and shield

FIRST SET: Wonder Woman Warrior Battle
SET NUMBER: 76075
YEAR: 2017

Tiara is printed on head piece instead of being molded to hair

Hair piece can be swapped for a blue hood and cape

Leather sword harness

Bulletproof bracelets on both arms

DID YOU KNOW?

These two variants are based on Wonder Woman's character in the movies *Wonder Woman* (2017) and *Batman v Superman: Dawn of Justice* (2016).

FACE TO FACE

With her trusty sword and a shield with an eagle motif, Wonder Woman's 2016 minifigure knows her clash with Lex Luthor will mean the difference between war and the dawn of justice!

WONDER WOMAN USES lightning-fast reflexes to deflect bullets with her armor bracelets and is ready for whatever Ares can throw at her. In her battle with the God of War and longtime enemy of the Amazons, she is the star of the show.

WONDER WOMAN

HEIR OF ASTERIA

Eagle-headed helmet

Regal armor is a tribute to Diana's homeland, Themyscira

Wings enable Wonder Woman to fly

DID YOU KNOW?

Asteria's armor was created so she could hold back humans while the Amazons fled to the safety of Themyscira.

VITAL STATS

LIKES: Ancient artifacts
DISLIKES: Misuse of modern technology
FRIENDS: Steve Trevor
FOES: The Cheetah, Maxwell Lord
SKILLS: Flight
GEAR: Winged suit, Lasso of Truth

FIRST SET: Wonder Woman vs. Cheetah
SET NUMBER: 76157
YEAR: 2020

FIGHT AND FLIGHT

Wonder Woman armors up to fly to the island headquarters of the villainous Maxwell Lord. His bunker has a high-tech transmitter tower that threatens the world.

DIANA PRINCE NOW works in the American Museum of Natural History. She always seeks peace, but she won't shy away from a fight when needed. Fortunately, she has just the thing for the job—the warrior Asteria's head-to-toe golden armor.

LIVELY, BOLD, AND FEARLESS, Etta Candy is best pals with Wonder Woman. An ordinary human but an extraordinary friend, she helps Diana Prince navigate the "World of Man." They go way back to 1942, soon after Diana's arrival from Paradise Island.

1940s-style hairdo

VITAL STATS

LIKES: Sweets
DISLIKES: Missing out on the action
FRIENDS: Wonder Woman
FOES: The Cheetah
SKILLS: Leadership
GEAR: None

FIRST SET: Wonder Woman
SET NUMBER: 77906
YEAR: 2020

Double-sided face has an anxious smile and an anguished wail

Short leg piece because Etta is shorter than Wonder Woman

COVER STORY
Etta watches on while her best friend battles with The Cheetah in this LEGO® recreation of the cover image from *Wonder Woman #6* (September 1943). The set was a DC FanDome exclusive.

STEVE TREVOR

US AIR FORCE ACE

WORLDLY AND BATTLE-HARDENED Captain Steve Trevor thinks he has seen it all, but he is in for a surprise. When his jet crashes near Themyscira, Wonder Woman rescues him from the sea, and he is the first foreigner to step on the Amazonians' homeland.

Flight goggles

Helmet can be swapped for a dashing hair piece

Ribbed knitwear for warmth

Army-issue flight jacket

VITAL STATS

LIKES: Loop the loop and other aerobatic maneuvers
DISLIKES: Bailing out in the sea
FRIENDS: Wonder Woman
FOES: Ares
SKILLS: Piloting his jet
GEAR: Fighter plane

FIRST SET: Wonder Woman Warrior Battle
SET NUMBER: 76075
YEAR: 2017

PILOT EPISODE

Steve Trevor serves the US Air Force in his fighter jet, but unknown to him, his orders are coming from Ares, the God of War. Wonder Woman realizes Ares's role and defeats him.

VIXEN

FORCE OF NATURE

DID YOU KNOW?

Vixen's minifigure is based on her character from the *Arrowverse* TV series *DC's Legends of Tomorrow*.

CRAWLING UP A wall like a spider? Enduring extreme cold like a seal? Charging with the force of an elephant? These and other animal-spirit powers are second nature to Amaya Jiwe—as long as she wears the Anansi Totem.

Anansi Totem is the source of Vixen's powers, but it can be removed

VITAL STATS

LIKES: Brute force
DISLIKES: Time pirates
FRIENDS: The Atom
FOES: Anyone disrupting the time line
SKILLS: Channeling animal spirits
GEAR: None

Protective suit is extremely durable

FIRST SET: Vixen
SET NUMBER: SDCC2017
YEAR: 2017

ANIMAL MAGIC

With her animal spirit powers, Vixen joins the Legends of Tomorrow—a time-traveling group that protects the time line. Amaya Jiwe goes on to become the grandmother of the second Vixen, Mari McCabe.

CYBORG
MECHANICAL WHIZZ

Hair is attached to helmet piece

DID YOU KNOW?

On the cover of the 1982 comic *Tales of the New Teen Titans #1*, Cyborg is shown breaking purple chains.

More flesh is revealed on this minifigure than on Cyborg's previous variants

OUT ON A LIMB

The three earlier Cyborg minifigures have solid pants, variations in printing, and helmets with full chinstraps. The 2017 variant has an arm with a blaster rather than a minifigure hand.

VITAL STATS

LIKES: Justice League
DISLIKES: Rusty parts
FRIENDS: Superman, Green Arrow, Hawkman, Beast Boy
FOES: Darkseid
SKILLS: Cybernetic attacks
GEAR: Purple chains

FIRST SET: Collectible LEGO DC Super Heroes Minifigures Series
SET NUMBER: 71026
YEAR: 2020

Metallic Utility Belt matches armor

Leg printing reveals extensive metallic parts

WHEN VIC STONE was injured, his father rebuilt him as half man, half machine. Becoming Cyborg, he gained the ability to interface with computers, although rumors that he uses his advanced cybernetics to cheat while playing Batman at video games aren't true!

BEAST VS. BIRD

A real prankster, Beast Boy loves to play practical jokes on his teammates. However, as his alternate face shows, he wasn't so happy to find himself tricked and trapped in a duck prison by The Penguin.

Beast Boy's pointed ears are molded to his hair piece

Grinning face

Distinctive purple outfit

Dark-green hands

VITAL STATS

LIKES: Playing tricks
DISLIKES: Being locked up
FRIENDS: Robin, Starfire, Batman
FOES: The Penguin, The Joker, Harley Quinn, Poison Ivy
SKILLS: Shapeshifting
GEAR: Staff, handcuffs, lock

FIRST SET: Jokerland
SET NUMBER: 76035
YEAR: 2015

GARFIELD LOGAN IS a bit of every animal. The Teen Titan can transform himself into any bird or beast, thanks to a special serum that saved him from a toxic animal bite as a child. Unfortunately, it left him with green-colored skin as well!

179

STARFIRE
ALIEN PRINCESS

VITAL STATS

LIKES: Fun
DISLIKES: Misery
FRIENDS: Robin, Beast Boy, Batman
FOES: Poison Ivy, Harley Quinn, The Joker, The Penguin
SKILLS: Flight
GEAR: Starbolt energy

FIRST SET: Jokerland
SET NUMBER: 76035
YEAR: 2015

Long, flowing purple hair

Double-sided head shows an anxious expression

Starbolt energy blasts made from green LEGO plate pieces

STAR BRIGHT
When The Joker took over the Gotham City Funfair, Starfire and the Teen Titans flew to Batman's aid. Plants usually like light, but Poison Ivy wasn't so keen on Starfire's starbolts!

THE DAUGHTER OF THE
Tamaran king and queen, Princess Koriand'r absorbs solar energy through her skin and converts it to the power she needs to fly and blast emerald energy bolts from her hands. Now, she fights alongside Robin in the Teen Titans.

A STING IN THE TAIL

New double-knot hair piece

Bug-eyed flight goggles

STING WITH BLING

They say lightning never strikes in the same place twice, but it does if Bumblebee is after you. She zaps double bolts of lightning energy that sting like a bee.

High-tech battlesuit

VITAL STATS

LIKES: Honey
DISLIKES: Honey traps
FRIENDS: Teen Titans
FOES: Bumbling villains
SKILLS: Energy generation
GEAR: 2 electrical weapons

FIRST SET: Collectible LEGO DC Super Heroes Minifigures Series
SET NUMBER: 71026
YEAR: 2020

QUEEN OF SCIENCE, Karen Beecher invents her own Super Hero costume that gives her the power to generate energy, shrink, and fly. The suit really is the bee's knees. She joins the Teen Titans and later works for S.T.A.R. Labs.

181

CHAPTER SIX

JUSTICE LEAGUE BEWARE!

DARKSEID

CAN YOU CATCH MY CANNONBALLS?

BIG-HITTING SUPER HEROES like the Justice League attract Super-Villains who hit big. Some have personal vendettas against particular Super Heroes, but others are just out to cause as much chaos as they can. One thing is for sure ... The Justice League had better watch out!

PRANKS A LOT!

VITAL STATS

LIKES: Tricking people
DISLIKES: Being tricked
FRIENDS: Captain Cold
FOES: The Flash
SKILLS: Telling jokes
GEAR: Anti-gravity boots

FIRST SET: LEGO® DC Comics Super Heroes Justice League: Attack of the Legion of Doom! DVD movie
YEAR: 2015

No other LEGO® minifigure has hair this color

DID YOU KNOW?

Axel Walker is the second Trickster. The first was James Jesse, who also had many a clash with The Flash.

Two-color arms suggest T-shirt sleeves

Belt and braces lined with gadget pouches

Checkered pattern continues on side of legs

REAR AXEL

The Trickster's belt and suspenders printing continues on his back, adding more pouches in which he can store twisted trick items such as itching powder and exploding rubber chickens!

AXEL WALKER IS no ordinary teenage villain. As the Trickster, he uses practical jokes and wacky gadgets to commit his crimes and has invented a pair of anti-gravity boots that let him run through the air to escape The Flash.

GORILLA GRODD
GOING APE

ONCE GRODD WAS JUST another gorilla living in a rainforest. That was until a crashed alien spacecraft gave the great ape hyperintelligence. Now Grodd is able to telepathically control minds!

Mind control equipment

VITAL STATS

LIKES: Bananas
DISLIKES: Rotten fruit
FRIENDS: Captain Cold
FOES: The Flash, Batman, Wonder Woman
SKILLS: Mind control
GEAR: Banana

FIRST SET: Gorilla Grodd Goes Bananas
SET NUMBER: 76026
YEAR: 2015

JUST BANANAS
If there's one thing Gorilla Grodd loves, it's trying to take over the world. But if there's another thing he loves, it's nice tasty bananas. So much so that he attacks this unsuspecting truck driver.

DID YOU KNOW?
Gorilla Grodd made his comic debut in issue 106 of The Flash back in 1959.

DARKSEID

OVERSIZE ALIEN OVERLORD

VITAL STATS

LIKES: Conquering
DISLIKES: Justice League
FRIENDS: None
FOES: Superman, Cyborg, Green Arrow, Hawkman
SKILLS: Invading planets
GEAR: Hover Destroyer

FIRST SET: Darkseid Invasion
SET NUMBER: 76028
YEAR: 2015

Cracked gray skin

Darkseid's red eyes can launch laser beams

Huge gripping hand

CANNONBALL CHAOS

Darkseid's invasion starts in Metropolis, when the alien overlord plays skittles with skyscrapers, blasting cannonballs from a Hover Launcher enlarged for his oversize form.

THE TYRANNICAL ruler of Apokolips has set his eyes on the rest of the universe. Invulnerable to anything but his own eye-beams, Darkseid is super-strong and resourceful. Nothing will stop his takeover plans.

CAPTAIN COLD

HOODED HOODLUM

Despite his name, Captain Cold likes to wrap up warm

Cold eyes hidden by thick goggles

Coolly confident grin

DID YOU KNOW?

Captain Cold is the leader of a criminal gang called the Rogues. Its members include the Trickster.

PLOWING ON

With a snow cone in one hand and his freeze gun in the other, a short-legged Captain Cold uses this Mighty Micros snowplow to find his way through the ice.

LOOK OUT—there's an ice age coming! Ice-cool villain Captain Cold makes his own microclimate with his fearsome freeze gun and his frosty manner. He would love to fast-freeze The Flash in a big block of ice!

VITAL STATS

LIKES: Fishing
DISLIKES: Dry land
FRIENDS: None
FOES: Aquaman, Mera
SKILLS: Deep-sea diving
GEAR: Submarine, sword

FIRST SET: Black Manta Strike
SET NUMBER: 76095
YEAR: 2018

There's no minifigure head beneath that oversize helmet

Tubes take air into the helmet from the tank on his back

Scuba suit printing continues on the back

SUPER SUIT
Although Black Manta has no superpowers, he's a formidable foe. His 2015 minifigure wears a variant of his custom-made scuba suit that enables him to survive the extreme pressure of the seabed, fire lasers from his eyes, and shoot electric bolts.

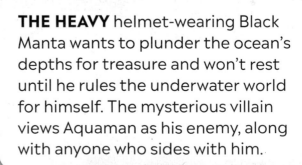

THE HEAVY helmet-wearing Black Manta wants to plunder the ocean's depths for treasure and won't rest until he rules the underwater world for himself. The mysterious villain views Aquaman as his enemy, along with anyone who sides with him.

DOOMSDAY

REPEAT OFFENDER

DOOMED TO ENDURE cruel experiments by the scientist Bertron, Doomsday has died again and again but always comes back stronger. The genetically honed monster has a bone to pick with the Justice League, and he won't rest until they are destroyed— even if he's destroyed first.

Ponytail LEGO piece used in white for the first time

Furry eyebrows

Neck brace with six bone spurs

Remains of fur on chest

Short Mighty Micro legs haven't yet evolved to maximum height

VITAL STATS

LIKES: Destroying stuff
DISLIKES: Reruns
FRIENDS: Doomsayers
FOES: Wonder Woman
SKILLS: Coming back to life
GEAR: Club, vehicle with flames

FIRST SET: Mighty Micros: Wonder Woman vs. Doomsday
SET NUMBER: 76070
YEAR: 2017

DOOM AND GLOOM
Make no bones about Doomsday's determination to destroy Wonder Woman. He attacks her Invisible Jet in his highly evolved vehicle, complete with bones and searing flames.

VITAL STATS

LIKES: Being Bad
DISLIKES: Clark Kent
FRIENDS: The Bizarro League
FOES: Superman
SKILLS: Freeze vision and heat breath
GEAR: None

FIRST SET: Bizarro
SET NUMBER: COMCON022
YEAR: 2012

Chalk-white and wrinkled skin

Reversed S-shield in muted colors

A medallion made of rock helps Bizarro remember his own name

BACK-SEAT DRIVER

A shorter-legged Bizarro angrily drives his reverse-built Mighty Micro car. But like everything in his topsy-turvy life, he drives it backward and in the wrong direction. Don't bet on him throwing his Kryptonite the right way.

DID YOU KNOW?

In LEGO® *Batman™ 3: Beyond Gotham*, Bizarro stole Luthor's duplication ray to make Bizarro versions of the Justice League.

CREATED BY EVIL GENIUS Lex Luthor, this muddled clone of Superman gets everything the wrong way around. Childish and prone to throwing tantrums, Bizarro sees life in reverse. For him, good is bad and bad is good.

SINESTRO

FALLEN LANTERN

Double-sided head with a snarling face on the back

Three blue stripes printed on each sleeve

Bright-pink face unique to Sinestro

Black printing continues on the back of the minifigure

Symbol of the Sinestro Corps

VITAL STATS

LIKES: Absolute power
DISLIKES: Hal Jordan
FRIENDS: The Sinestro Corps
FOES: Green Lantern, Batman
SKILLS: Lantern-napping
GEAR: Yellow Lantern, Power Ring

FIRST SET: Collectible LEGO DC Super Heroes Minifigures Series
SET NUMBER: 71026
YEAR: 2020

ONCE CONSIDERED the greatest Green Lantern of them all, Sinestro was actually using his great powers to enslave alien races. Stripped of his power ring, Sinestro formed the evil Sinestro Corps and became the Green Lantern's sworn enemy.

LANTERN LIFTOFF

In his original yellow suit, Sinestro's minifigure stole Hal Jordan's Lantern and placed it in a protective cage. It has just enough space for one object—either the Lantern or Sinestro himself!

Full-body catsuit with furry ears

This is the only The Cheetah minifigure without a hair piece

CHEATING AND STEALING

Embracing all things cheetah, Priscilla embarks on a life of crime and a cat-and-mouse game with Wonder Woman. She is determined to live up to her new name, The Cheetah, and her surname, Rich.

DID YOU KNOW?

Two villains have gone by the name The Cheetah: Priscilla Rich and scientist Barbara Ann Minerva.

Tail attaches between torso and leg pieces

PRISCILLA RICH is one catty woman. Haunted by her jealousy of Diana Prince and bent on revenge, the petty thief makes herself a spotty cat outfit from an old cheetah pelt. Wonder Woman had better beware: The Cheetah has her claws out.

VITAL STATS

LIKES: Stealing, revenge
DISLIKES: Getting caught
FRIENDS: Rich people
FOES: Wonder Woman
SKILLS: Cat burglary
GEAR: Bag of swag

FIRST SET: Collectible LEGO DC Super Heroes Minifigures Series
SET NUMBER: 71026
YEAR: 2020

THE CHEETAH

FURIOUS FELINE

VITAL STATS

LIKES: Studying science
DISLIKES: Diana Prince
FRIENDS: Maxwell Lord
FOES: Wonder Woman
SKILLS: Stalking her prey
GEAR: None

FIRST SET: Wonder Woman vs. Cheetah
SET NUMBER: 76157
YEAR: 2020

Barbara's long hair remains after her transformation

RELENTLESS HUNTRESS
The Cheetah's 2018 minifigure wears black clothes over spotty cat-print skin, and she flashes her teeth in a fierce grin. She battles Wonder Woman with her spear to keep her claws on a stolen Energy Infuser

Superpowered claws can rip almost anything

Sleek new fur print in subdued colors

DID YOU KNOW?
The white-haired The Cheetah minifigure is based on the character's appearance in the 2020 Wonder Woman movie *WW 1984*.

DR. BARBARA ANN MINERVA was just a clever scientist until she pounced at the chance of a new life as a superpowered villain. Bestowed with mystical powers, Barbara Ann transforms into a ruthless cheetah, intent on Wonder Woman's destruction.

PARADEMON

ALIEN HENCHMAN

VITAL STATS

LIKES: Winning
DISLIKES: Losing
FRIENDS: More Parademons
FOES: Batman, The Flash
SKILLS: Overwhelming the enemy with sheer numbers
GEAR: Stud-shooter

FIRST SET: Knightcrawler Tunnel Attack
SET NUMBER: 76086
YEAR: 2017

Armor resistant to most weapons and energy assaults

Fiery insides glow through cracks in armor

Wings are not natural—they are part of the armored suit

THESE DIABOLICAL SHOCK troops are the foot soldiers of evil alien masters. They make formidable opponents, not just because of their superhuman strength and stamina but because they regenerate their injured bodies.

DEMON SEAMAN

Water is no obstacle to Parademons. A yellow-and-blue one swoops on the underwater kingdom of Atlantis in search of the powerful Mother Box that was hidden there for Earth's protection.

FEUDING FOES

VITAL STATS

NAME: Killer Frost
LIKES: Draining heat from others, especially Firestorm
DISLIKES: The cold
FRIENDS: Reverse Flash
FOES: The Flash, Cyborg
SKILLS: Ice powers
GEAR: Ice car, Ice Power Bursts

FIRST SET: Speed Force Freeze Pursuit
SET NUMBER: 76098
YEAR: 2018

Hair has been frozen white

Snowflake decoration

FOR SOME VILLAINS, it's personal. Killer Frost has it in for Firestorm; Maxwell Lord has a vendetta against Wonder Woman; and Ocean Master is Aquaman's evil half brother.

Silver LEGO helmet is unique to this minifigure

VITAL STATS

NAME: Ocean Master
LIKES: The sea
DISLIKES: The surface world
FRIENDS: None
FOES: All sentient beings
SKILLS: Wielding his powerful Trident
GEAR: Trident

FIRST SET: Batman Batsub and the Underwater Clash
SET NUMBER: 76116
YEAR: 2019

Same hair piece as the 1960s-styled Bruce Wayne minifigure

VITAL STATS

NAME: Maxwell Lord
LIKES: World domination
DISLIKES: Watching the world go by
FRIENDS: The Cheetah
FOES: Wonder Woman
SKILLS: Business
GEAR: None

FIRST SET: Wonder Woman vs. Cheetah
SET NUMBER: 76157
YEAR: 2020

Torso print shared with entrepreneur Bruce Wayne

Physique evolved to live underwater

Smart suit of business tycoon

 Penguin Random House

Project Editor Lisa Stock
Senior Designer David McDonald
Designers James McKeag, Elena Jarmosh
Senior Controller Lloyd Robertson
Prodution Editor Siu Yin Chan
Managing Editor Paula Regan
Managing Art Editor Jo Connor
Publishing Director Mark Searle

Additional Photography Markos Chouris,
Christopher Chouris, and Gary Ombler

This American Edition, 2022
First American Edition, 2016
Published in the United States by DK Publishing
1450 Broadway, Suite 801, New York, NY 10018

Page design copyright © 2022 Dorling Kindersley Limited
DK, a Division of Penguin Random House LLC

22 23 24 25 26 10 9 8 7 6 5 4 3 2
001–326983–May/22

LEGO, the LEGO logo, the Minifigure, and the Brick
and Knob configurations are trademarks and/or
copyrights of the LEGO Group. ©2022 The LEGO Group.
All rights reserved. Manufactured by Dorling Kindersley
under license from the LEGO Group.

Copyright © 2022 DC Comics. All DC Characters and
elements © & ™ DC Comics. (s22)

All rights reserved. Without limiting the rights under the
copyright reserved above, no part of this publication may be
reproduced, stored in or introduced into a retrieval system,
or transmitted, in any form, or by any means (electronic,
mechanical, photocopying, recording, or otherwise),
without the prior written permission of the copyright owner.
Published in Great Britain by Dorling Kindersley Limited

A catalog record for this book is available from
the Library of Congress.
ISBN 978-0-7440-5458-3
ISBN 978-0-7440-6104-8 (library edition)

DK books are available at special discounts when purchased in bulk
for sales promotions, premiums, fund-raising, or educational use.
For details, contact: DK Publishing Special Markets,
1450 Broadway, Suite 801, New York, NY 10018
SpecialSales@dk.com

Printed and bound in China

For the curious
www.LEGO.com
www.dk.com

ACKNOWLEDGMENTS

Batman created by Bob Kane with Bill Finger

Superman created by Jerry Siegel and Joe Shuster
By special arrangement with the Jerry Siegel family

Supergirl based on characters created by Jerry Siegel
and Joe Shuster
By special arrangement with the Jerry Siegel Family

Wonder Woman created by William Moulton Marston

Aquaman created by Paul Norris and Mort Weisinger

DK would like to thank Randi Sørensen, Tess Howarth,
Paul Hansford, Martin Leighton Lindhardt, and Anna
Matvienko at the LEGO Group; Ben Harper, Thomas Zellers,
and Melanie Swartz at Warner Bros.; Elizabeth Dowsett,
Cavan Scott, and Simon Hugo for their writing;
and Jennette ElNaggar for proofreading.

MIX
Paper from
responsible sources
FSC™ C018179

This book was made with Forest
Stewardship Council ™ certified
paper—one small step in DK's
commitment to a sustainable future.
For more information go to
www.dk.com/our-green-pledge